"He's four years old?"

Sarah nodded but didn't speak.

Shock was giving way to incredulous acceptance, followed swiftly by a bright flame of anger.

"And you never told me? Four years and you never told me I had a son?"

Sarah flinched at his angry demand as if she'd taken a body blow. She'd hoped against hope that they would never have this conversation, prayed that somehow God would spare her this. Hadn't she suffered enough?

"I'm not sure you do have a son, Joshua."

"What does that mean?" he bit out. "If he's four years old and he was born around Christmas, then he's mine."

"I'm not sure that you're the father," Sarah said.

Stunned, Josh felt as if she'd hit him in the chest with a two-by-four. He could barely breathe.

Dear Reader,

Fall is to be savored for all its breathtaking glory—and a spectacular October lineup awaits at Special Edition!

For years, readers have treasured Tracy Sinclair's captivating romances…and October commemorates her fiftieth Silhouette book! To help celebrate this wonderful author's crowning achievement, be sure to check out *The Princess Gets Engaged*— an enthralling romance that finds American tourist Megan Delaney in a royal mess when she masquerades as a princess and falls hopelessly in love with the charming Prince Nicholas.

This month's THAT'S MY BABY! title is by Lois Faye Dyer. *He's Got His Daddy's Eyes* is a poignant reunion story about hope, the enduring power of love and how one little boy works wonders on two broken hearts.

Nonstop romance continues as three veteran authors deliver enchanting stories. Check out award-winning author Marie Ferrarella's adorable tale about mismatched lovers when a blue-blooded heroine hastily marries a blue-collar carpenter in *Wanted: Husband, Will Train.* And what's an amnesiac triplet to do when she washes up on shore and right into the arms of a brooding billionaire? Find out in *The Mysterious Stranger,* when Susan Mallery's engaging TRIPLE TROUBLE series splashes to a finish! Reader favorite Arlene James serves up a tender story about unexpected love in *The Knight, The Waitress and the Toddler*— book four in our FROM BUD TO BLOSSOM promo series.

Finally, October's WOMAN TO WATCH is debut author Lisette Belisle, who unfolds an endearing romance between an innocent country girl and a gruff drifter in *Just Jessie.*

I hope you enjoy these books, and all of the stories to come!

Sincerely,

Tara Gavin, Senior Editor

Please address questions and book requests to:
Silhouette Reader Service
U.S.: 3010 Walden Ave., P.O. Box 1325, Buffalo, NY 14269
Canadian: P.O. Box 609, Fort Erie, Ont. L2A 5X3

LOIS FAYE DYER

HE'S GOT HIS DADDY'S EYES

Silhouette®

SPECIAL ▼ EDITION®

Published by Silhouette Books

America's Publisher of Contemporary Romance

For my parents, Steve and Ruby Jacobson,
and my siblings, Jeanie, Bernard,
Shirley, Elsie and Carol

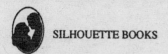 SILHOUETTE BOOKS

ISBN 0-373-24129-1

HE'S GOT HIS DADDY'S EYES

Copyright © 1997 by Lois Faye Dyer

Books by Lois Faye Dyer

Silhouette Special Edition

Lonesome Cowboy #1038
He's Got His Daddy's Eyes #1129

LOIS FAYE DYER

Winner of the 1989-1990 *Romantic Times* Reviewer's Choice Award for Best New Series Author, Lois Faye Dyer lives on Washington State's beautiful Puget Sound with her husband and their yellow Lab, Maggie Mae. She ended a career as a paralegal and Superior Court clerk to fulfill a lifelong dream to write. When she's not involved in writing, she enjoys long walks on the beach with her husband, watching musical and Western movies from the 1940s and 1950s and, most of all, indulging her passionate addiction to reading. This is her ninth published novel.

Dear Reader,

I adore babies, because babies grow into children, and children are amazing. They bring joy to our lives with their infectious laughter and spontaneous, throat-strangling hugs and kisses. They inspire awe in our hearts as we watch them thrive, stretch their horizons and grow to young adulthood under our guidance. Unfortunately, babies don't come with maintenance manuals, but if we're lucky, they forgive our blunders and love us anyway.

Children are an integral part of a family, and what "family" means to different people is at the very heart of the books I write. In the story you are about to read, Joshua Hightower lost his family, and his heart, when Sarah Drummond walked out of his life. When all her hope was gone, Sarah, like so many other mothers since time began, found the will to rebuild her life because of her son, J.J. And for the love of J.J. and Sarah, Joshua Hightower finds the strength to risk his heart one more time.

I hope you enjoy reading Josh and Sarah's story as much as I enjoyed writing it. I wish you peace and joy, and children, in your life to love and be loved by.

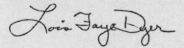

Chapter One

"Sarah Drummond's back in town."

Joshua Hightower went stock-still, his fingers closing into a fist over the handle of the plastic gallon container of milk.

Unaware of the shock she'd just dealt to the big cowboy standing behind her, Mrs. Applegate continued gossiping to the small market's checkout clerk.

"You could have knocked me over with a feather when I ran into her at the bank a few minutes ago. I'm sure I don't know what took that girl so long to get here. Her mother was hospitalized with a stroke three days ago." The little old lady sniffed disapprovingly. She handed the clerk her money and gathered up her bag. "Thank goodness my children aren't so thoughtless."

"Right." The clerk smiled at the little lady.

Josh waited impatiently until the gossipy woman moved on before he set the container of milk down on the counter and shoved one hand into his jeans pocket for money.

"Afternoon, Josh," the clerk said cheerfully. "Haven't seen you in a while. You been out of town?"

"Yeah, just got back," Josh replied brusquely. "How much do I owe you?"

The woman flicked him a wary glance and quickly rang up his total.

Josh handed her the money and muttered a brief goodbye before escaping the small convenience-store-cum-gas station. He stepped outside and the midafternoon heat hit him full force. He yanked open the door to his dusty pickup, tossed the gallon of milk across the seat to the passenger side and slid beneath the wheel, slamming the door behind him.

"Damn." Josh lifted the Stetson he wore and thrust his fingers through coal black, heat-dampened hair in an absentminded gesture of long habit. "She's back."

He resettled the hat and stared blankly out the windshield while waves of anger and pain buffeted him. He didn't see the glass-fronted store; instead, the image of Sarah Drummond's delicate features—

blue eyes, blond hair and lush, smiling mouth—floated in front of him in painful, brilliant Technicolor.

A carload of teenagers pulled in to the parking space beside him, their shouts and noisy laughter jolting him back to the present. He twisted the key in the ignition and backed the truck out into the street.

It was just his luck that the traffic light turned from green to amber seconds before he reached the intersection on Butte Creek's Main Street.

"Hell," he growled in disgust. He was tired, through-to-the-bone weary. He'd driven straight through from Colorado after delivering a quarter horse mare to her new owner. The four hours of sleep he'd grabbed at a rest stop hadn't been enough to make up for what he'd missed in the past three days. Neither had the gallons of coffee he'd drunk. He needed hot food, a shower and at least eighteen hours of uninterrupted sleep. Given the workload that was waiting for him at home, he knew he didn't have a prayer of sleeping anywhere near that many hours.

His fingers drummed impatiently against the steering wheel, and he rolled his shoulders to stretch the tense muscles. His gaze flicked idly over a woman who'd stepped off the curb and started across the street. He registered her slender figure, her unusual silver-blond hair, and moved beyond to the bank on the corner before snapping back. He stiffened, his fingers closing punishingly over the steering wheel.

"Sarah." He wasn't aware he'd said her name aloud. He was too busy absorbing the shock of seeing her after five long years.

She'd cut her hair. Gone was the long, thick mane that had fallen to her waist five years before. Now it was sideparted and cut short to swing forward and brush against her jawline, where it gleamed with the satiny sheen of silver under the hot caress of the sun. Dark sunglasses hid her eyes, but the short, straight nose, full lips and stubborn jaw were undisguisable, as was the curvy shape inside a calf-length yellow sundress that left her arms and shoulders bare.

A gust of pure rage shook him.

Damn you, he thought fiercely. *Why couldn't you have gotten older, uglier, heavier—anything but better?*

Sarah passed within three feet of the front bumper of his pickup. Josh tensed, anticipating the moment when she would glance up and see him, but she never even looked at the truck. He wasn't sure whether he was relieved or irritated that she didn't realize he was watching her.

She disappeared into the drugstore on the opposite corner, and he stared at the empty doorway, struggling to deal with the complex mix of emotions roiling beneath the anger. Behind him, a horn

honked and he looked up to find that the traffic light
had turned green.

"All right, all right," he snarled at the impatient
driver. He shifted the pickup into gear and crossed
the intersection, heading west out of Butte Creek
toward the Rocking D. He wondered if Sarah knew
that the estate trustee, George Ankrum, had leased
the outbuildings and acres of the Drummond spread
to him and Zach Colby. Or if she knew that he was
living in the old foreman's house beyond the spring.

He shrugged, his jaw tightening, his eyes narrowing beneath the brim of his Stetson.

He didn't care whether she knew or not, he told
himself grimly. He and Sarah Drummond were an-
cient history; they had been for five long years.
Whatever hopes he may have clung to when she
disappeared had been shattered and buried when
he'd received a letter from her a year later. She'd
wished him well, told him that there was no future
for them and that she hoped he'd be happy.

Happy. Josh wasn't sure he knew what that word
meant anymore. He'd managed to put the pieces of
his life back together, partly by sealing memories
of Sarah in an untouchable part of his empty heart,
and partly by focusing his entire life on his horses.

And that's the way it's going to stay, he thought
grimly. *If she's only here because her mother's ill,
she'll be gone when Mrs. Drummond recovers.
She'll undoubtedly stay at her mother's house in*

town and not come near the ranch, so it's unlikely we'll run into each other.

Dust from the gravel road ballooned behind the wheels of the pickup, and the June sun was hot on his arm where it lay on the rolled-down window. Even behind sunglasses, Josh's eyes narrowed against the glare, but he welcomed the distraction. Thinking about Sarah Drummond was an exercise in frustration and painful futility. Instead, he forced himself to focus on the long list of work that awaited him at the ranch.

"Mama? Mama, are you awake?" Sarah asked softly, reluctant to disturb her mother. Seeing Patricia Drummond lying motionless in the hospital bed had been a shock. She'd never known her mother to leave the house looking less than perfectly groomed and stylishly dressed. Now her thin figure was clothed in a cotton hospital gown, a white sheet covering her to her waist. Her arms were frail below the short sleeves of the gown, the tube taped to the back of her left hand an indignity. She wore no makeup to highlight the sculpted bone structure or to conceal the age lines on her face, and her hair was simply brushed back from her temples. The soft gold strands, threaded with silver, did little to add color to her pale face.

The indomitable force of will that was so much a part of Patricia Drummond's makeup was missing. Sarah choked back the need to shake her mother awake and find out if the essential force that had driven Patricia all her life was truly gone.

Pale gold lashes fluttered and slowly lifted. Sarah searched the blue eyes; the confusion and fear that she found there clutched at her heart.

"Mama?"

"Sarah." Patricia spoke slowly, with effort, the word slurred.

"Yes, Mama." Relief that Patricia recognized her flooded Sarah, but it was tempered with worry. The left side of her mother's face pulled downward, and her lips had struggled to shape the single word she spoke. "How are you feeling?"

"Fi-ine. Mar'gret?"

"I telephoned her, Mother. She said she doesn't know if she can get leave from work." Sarah saw the disappointment that replaced her mother's brief surge of hope, and silently cursed her irresponsible sister. She didn't think it necessary to tell Patricia that her oldest daughter hadn't even been home the two times Sarah had tried to reach her at her apartment in Los Angeles. Margaret's twelve-year-old daughter, Caitlin, had relayed messages between her mother and her aunt.

"I'm sure she'll be here if she can, and as soon as she can," Sarah added. She was rewarded with a slight, lopsided grimace from Patricia, but knew from the weary acceptance in her eyes that Patricia wasn't fooled. "I've spoken with your doctor. He tells me that the prognosis for your recovery is good and that as soon as the episodes of arrhythmia stop, you'll be moved to a convalescent center.''

"Go home.''

For the first time, Sarah saw a resurgence of the strong-willed mother she knew.

"Mama, you can't go home, not right now,'' she said gently. "Even if the doctor released you, it will be a month or more before the carpenters and plumbers are finished at your house.''

The bewildered confusion on her mother's face was enlightening. "You're having your house remodeled and you've been staying with Dorothy, remember?''

The hesitation before her mother nodded told Sarah that the ripped-up bathroom flooring and the living room's exposed wall studs were not something Patricia remembered. The doctor had warned her that Patricia's memory was shaky, at best.

"By the time you're ready to go home, your house should be finished,'' Sarah said soothingly.

Patricia frowned and stirred, her right hand gripping Sarah. "Hotel?'' she managed to say.

"Hotel? Oh, do you mean am I staying at the hotel?'' Her mother nodded and Sarah shook her head. "No, Mama. J.J. and I are staying at Aunt Molly's.''

Anger leapt to life in Patricia's eyes and her fingers clutched Sarah with amazing strength. She struggled to speak.

"What is it, Mama?'' Sarah searched her mother's face, realizing that there were two possible reasons her mother was upset. "Are you angry that I'm staying with Aunt Molly?"

Patricia shook her head.

"Then you must be upset because J.J. is here." Sarah didn't need her mother's frustrated nod to confirm what she'd already guessed. "I know I promised you that I wouldn't bring J.J. to Butte Creek, but when you became ill, it was impossible for me to keep that promise." She moved her hand to cover Patricia's, but her mother pulled away, glaring silently at her. Sarah refused to back down, and met that intimidating stare with unswerving calm. "J.J. is my son. Where I go, he goes. Do you want me to leave Butte Creek and go back to Great Falls?"

Patricia remained stubbornly silent. Sarah waited patiently. Finally, after several tense moments, Patricia reluctantly shook her head.

The hall door whooshed inward, propelled by a cheery, middle-aged nurse.

"Hello there." She bustled around the bed, nodding at Sarah before checking the contents of the upended bottle that was attached to the tube connected to Patricia's hand. "I'm sorry, dear, but I'm afraid you'll have to leave now. We're taking Mrs. Drummond downstairs for some tests."

Sarah nodded. "I understand. Dr. Silas explained that visiting time would be short this afternoon."

She stood and took her mother's hand in hers. "I'll be back tomorrow, Mama."

Patricia closed her eyes and turned her head away, her fingers lax and unresponsive to the squeeze Sarah gave them.

Sarah steeled herself against the quick spurt of hurt. She'd learned to turn a deaf ear to her mother's disapproval over the past four years, but hadn't yet become completely immune. She gave her mother's hand a last squeeze of affection, returned the nurse's sympathetic smile and left the room.

The bright sunlight assaulted her eyes the moment she stepped outside and Sarah winced, slipping her sunglasses onto her nose. The light intensified the headache that had been growing steadily stronger since she'd arrived at the hospital. Now it hammered at her temples.

Before I leave town, I've got to stop at the pharmacy and get some aspirin.

Although she'd parked her little economy car beneath the shade of an old box elder, the interior was stifling. Sarah twisted the key in the ignition and heaved a sigh of relief when the air conditioner kicked on. The rush of warm air quickly turned cooler, easing the pounding at her temples.

I'll see George Ankrum first. If he leased the ranch house, I don't know what I'll do.

Sarah had counted on staying at Patricia's home while she and J.J. were in Butte Creek. It had been a distinct shock to find it being renovated and completely uninhabitable. She'd taken J.J. to her aunt Molly and uncle Wes's when they'd arrived late the night before, but she knew she couldn't stay there indefinitely. The bewilderment and hurt on Wes's ruddy face when she'd stepped away from his hugs was a knife in her heart. She adored Wes Hildebrandt; that she hurt him when she avoided his spontaneous affection was unbearable.

Neither he nor Molly was going to understand when she told them that she and J.J. were going to stay at the Rocking D.

If I can stay at the Rocking D, she thought, and said a silent prayer that George Ankrum hadn't leased the ranch house with the rest of the ranch.

An hour later, after speaking with George at his office in the bank and crossing the street to collect extra-strength aspirin at the pharmacy, a relieved Sarah left town with the key to the Rocking D ranch house in her hand.

Although George had assured her that the empty ranch house was cleaned on a regular basis, she decided to stop by and check the house before going on to the Hildebrandt spread to collect J.J.

The well-oiled lock gave easily to her key. Inside, Sarah opened drapes and pulled off the sheets tossed over comfortable, well-worn furniture. A quick inspection of the kitchen further reassured her.

"Thank goodness Mr. Ankrum is so meticu-

lous,'' she murmured with relief. The house wasn't
only habitable, it was obviously well maintained.

She flipped a wall switch and was rewarded with
the glow from an overhead light. George had told
her he'd arranged a minimal basic fee with the elec-
tric company and used the electricity only during
the winter months to keep the water pipes from
freezing. The only utility not connected was the
telephone; Sarah knew she had to make phone service her first priority so the hospital could contact
her if necessary.

Satisfied that she and J.J. could spend the night,
she recrossed the living room and stepped out onto
the porch.

Her little red car was precisely where she'd left
it, but leaning against the near front fender was a
tall, broad-shouldered man in boots, jeans and a
cowboy hat.

It was the same uniform of dusty, casual work
clothes she'd often seen him wear five years before.

The man was Josh Hightower.

Sarah couldn't move. She couldn't breathe.
She'd thought she was prepared to see him again,
but she had assumed it would be in town. Perhaps
she'd pass him on the street. Perhaps she'd run into
him at the post office or the grocery store. Some-
time, somewhere—but not here, certainly not now.
Not the first day she was back, and not when she
was vulnerable, struggling to deal with the overload

of emotions brought about by seeing her mother so ill.

His eyes were still an intense, riveting turquoise, his hair the same coal black above his strong-boned, handsome face.

"What the hell are you doing here?"

Even across the yards that separated them, she could feel the cold anger that surrounded him, could see it raging in the hard stare that met hers unflinchingly, and in the stony, unforgiving set of his features.

He hates me.

She'd always known he would. She hadn't known how much it would hurt.

"What are *you* doing here?" she countered. Over the past five years she'd become adept at concealing her emotions; still, it took every ounce of control to force her gaze to meet his without wavering, to keep her expression calm and unruffled.

"I live here." He bit out the words.

"You live here?" Staggered, Sarah looked past him to the barn and corrals. "Where?"

"In the foreman's house."

"You can't." Sarah shook her head, dismay coloring her voice.

"Oh, yes, I can. I pay good money to rent this place—and I don't want you here. Leave."

"I can't."

"Sure you can. Go to your mother's place in town. Why aren't you there?"

"It's being remodeled."

"Then go to a hotel. You can't stay here."

The shock of seeing him was beginning to give way to anger. Sarah frowned at him. "Oh, yes, I can. George gave me the key. He also told me that the outbuildings and the land were leased to a company called ZJ Enterprises. That lease doesn't include the main house."

Josh glared at her and bit off a curse. "Well, I'm not leaving, and I damn sure don't want you here. Why don't you stay with Molly and Wes?"

Sarah didn't want to tell him why she couldn't deal with her beloved uncle on a daily basis—or any man, for that matter. "We'll be more comfortable here. There's more room."

"We?" Josh stiffened, his jaw hardened, and a muscle jumped in response. "Someone's with you?"

"Yes," Sarah replied. "He's—"

"Never mind." His hand lifted to slice the air in a silencing gesture. "Just stay the hell out of my way while you're here."

He pushed away from the car and turned abruptly, stalking away from her toward the barn. His big body radiated anger.

A headache throbbed at Sarah's temples. The extra-strength aspirin she'd taken before leaving Butte Creek had only begun to dull the hammering pain. Now it was back, stronger than ever, spurred on by the pressure of tears that burned behind her eyes.

She refused to let them fall. She'd cried buckets of tears over Josh Hightower. She refused to cry any more.

J.J. tugged on Sarah's sleeve, his thick-lashed, emerald eyes vivid beneath the shock of blond hair that fell across his brow. "Are we going to Grandma's house now?"

His voice interrupted her thoughts, and Sarah glanced down to find him chewing on a licorice whip.

"No, we're going to Grandpa John's house at the ranch," Sarah answered, resting a hand on J.J.'s jeans-clad knee.

"Who's Grandpa John?" he asked, his words garbled by a mouthful of licorice.

"Grandpa John was my daddy and Grandma Patricia's husband. I told you about him, remember?"

"Is he the grandpa that went to heaven?" J.J. asked.

"Yes." Sarah checked the wiggling little boy's seat-belt latch before he returned to the subject of his grandpa John's ranch.

"Are there horses and cows at Grandpa John's, Mommy?"

"Mmmhhh," Sarah said absentmindedly, her eyes narrowed against the rays from the setting sun slanting through the windshield. She'd been so preoccupied with the condition of the house and then stunned by her confrontation with Josh that she hadn't noticed if the pastures and corrals held stock. "I think so, J.J. Mr. Ankrum said the trust had leased the land and outbuildings to a horse-and-cattle operation, so the corrals and barn are being used."

"Good." J.J. nodded with satisfaction. "I like horses. What's a trust?" he asked abruptly.

Sarah glanced sideways at him, a rush of warm affection and delight filling her at the lively curiosity and intelligence in the bright look that met hers. "When Grandpa John died, he left the house in town to Grandma Patricia and the ranch to Aunt Margaret and me. But we were too young then to understand business and sign legal papers, so he asked Mr. Ankrum to do it for us. That's called a trust."

"Oh." J.J. seemed to accept the simplified explanation at face value and began to hum along with the Garth Brooks song on the radio.

J.J. was delighted once they reached the ranch. There were horses in the corrals, and more horses and cattle scattered across the pastures surrounding the Rocking D headquarters. Sarah had to collar the excited little boy to keep him from racing down the wide graveled driveway to the barn. She tugged her grumbling and protesting son beside her, then moved up the walkway and across the porch of the ranch house.

"Did you live here when you were a little girl,

Mommy?'' J.J. asked as he raced through the front door and up the stairs.

"Every summer until Grandpa John died," she answered, following him to the second floor.

"How come only summers?" His voice alternately faded and grew louder as he dashed in and out of the four bedrooms and the old-fashioned bathroom.

"Because my mother made us live in town during the winter so we could go to school."

"Why didn't you stay here and go to school?"

"Because it's a long way on a bus to get to the school in town, and she worried about us when the weather was snowy or icy in the wintertime."

J.J.'s questions continued through bathtime and being tucked into bed. He even interrupted the bedtime story Sarah was reading to him with new questions. J.J. was fascinated at how dramatically different the ranch was from the neat little duplex with its small fenced yard that they called home in Great Falls. By the time Sarah turned off his light, she was exhausted from the barrage of queries about Butte Creek, the ranch, his grandfather, and what she'd done as a little girl.

She didn't bother flicking on the light switch in the second-floor bedroom that had been hers since she was born. Moonlight poured through the windowpanes, and she crossed the room to slide the sash upward. The white cotton curtains stirred in the light breeze, and she lifted her face into the warm current of air, closing her eyes to breathe in the scents carried through the night. The heavy scent of alfalfa and dried-grass hay was underlaid with the faint, pungent smell of horses and cattle from the barn and corrals; intermixed was the fragrance of wild sage from the pastures and flat-topped buttes beyond the ranch buildings.

Sarah opened her eyes and leaned against the window frame, resting her aching head against the cool glass. The aspirin had reduced the pain to a slow, dull throb.

For five long years she'd alternately longed for and dreaded a return to Butte Creek and this land she'd loved since she was a child. After J.J. was born, when Patricia realized that she was adamant about keeping the baby instead of turning him over to an adoption agency, her mother had angrily demanded that she never embarrass her by returning to her hometown.

Sarah and her mother had always had a difficult relationship, but J.J.'s existence had opened a canyon between them. Although the stroke had stolen Patricia's ability to voice her displeasure, Sarah knew by the anger in her mother's eyes that she was upset that her friends would now discover that her daughter had a child but no husband.

But beyond her concerns about her mother, Sarah had alternately longed for and dreaded seeing Josh Hightower. Five years was a long time, but not long enough to dull her memory of the cowboy who'd been her first and only love. Events beyond her control had altered her life forever and destroyed her dreams of marriage and family. Still, part of her yearned for Josh. But she knew all too well that a life with him was impossible.

And after their confrontation this afternoon, she had no illusions about whether or not Josh remembered her with yearning or regrets for what might have been.

He hated her.

The quiet night was broken by the sound of a transmission downshifting, the rumbling purr of an engine growing louder as the vehicle neared the house.

Sarah straightened, her fingers fisting over the edge of the curtain.

The vehicle drew closer, rolling slowly past the front of the house. It was a ranch truck, four-wheel drive, dusty, the driver an indistinguishable black shape in the dark interior. The truck slowed, stopping just behind her little car where it was parked on the gravel outside the front yard gate. The pickup idled quietly for a long moment before it rolled forward, easing on past the house until it disappeared down the gravel lane, past the barn and corrals and beyond the edge of the grove of trees. The brake lights winked a bright red just before the engine shut off. Through the open window Sarah heard the distinctive, low sound of a truck door closing, and saw the dim glow of lights flicked on in the foreman's house just visible on the far side of the grove.

It didn't matter that the walls of two houses, the grove of trees and yards of land separated her from Josh. Her body, blessedly numb and encased in ice for the past five years, was awakening and remembering his. Unbidden and unwanted, memories of the gentleness of his touch and the feel of his mouth and body against hers flooded back to taunt her. She'd struggled so hard to come to terms with and accept what was left of her life, and thought she'd resigned herself to living without love. It was shattering to learn that one brief, angry encounter with Josh could set all her locked-away emotions clamoring to be free and destroy her hard-won peace of mind so easily.

Especially now that she knew beyond a shadow of a doubt that he hated her.

With a heavy sigh, she forced her fingers to ease their punishing grip on the curtain. Weariness overwhelmed her and she turned away from the window, pulling off her clothes and tugging an oversize T-shirt over her head before she tumbled into bed. The long drive across Montana from Great Falls to Butte Creek the day before, the difficult meeting with her mother and the doctor, followed by the confrontation with Josh, had combined to exhaust her. She was asleep only seconds after her head hit the pillow.

* * *

"What the hell is wrong with you this morning, Josh?" Murphy Redman slung a hand-tooled saddle into the bed of his pickup truck and slammed the tailgate shut.

"Nothing," Josh said flatly. He tossed a bridle on top of the saddle and turned back toward the open barn door.

"Now, just a dang minute." Murphy leaned his forearms on the top edge of the metal tailgate and fixed the younger man with a stern eye. "Don't be runnin' off. You know good and well I'm too old to chase you. Come back here."

Josh bit off a snarl and stalked back to the truck. Hands on hips, he glared at the white-haired man. "What do you want, Murphy?"

"I want to know what's got your tail in a twist this morning, that's what I want." Murphy pushed the brim of his straw cowboy hat higher. Worry added another crease to his weathered brow, and his black eyes were bright with concern. "Is there somethin' wrong with Baby?"

"No. There's nothing wrong with Baby."

Murphy was nonplussed. If Josh's quarter horse stud was healthy, then he was at a loss as to what could have caused the simmering temper that edged the younger man's tone and hazed the usual turquoise of his eyes to smoky blue. "One of the mares, then?"

"No."

Murphy ran a keen gaze over Josh's six-foot-two,

broad-shouldered, muscled length. "You don't look sick."

"I'm not sick," Josh said shortly.

"Then what the hell—"

"Hey, Josh."

Josh glanced over his shoulder to find his partner, Zach Colby, leading a sorrel mare toward him down the wide center aisle of the big horse barn.

"Yeah?"

"Did Walt say how long it would take him to weld the hitch on the horse trailer?"

"A day or two." Josh nodded toward the back bumper of his own truck. "He'll straighten the bumper and reweld the truck hitch on Thursday. I'll pick up the trailer then."

Murphy glanced at the dented bumper and the scratches in the tailgate's paint. "Is that what's got you in such a snit? Some danged fool rear-ended you on the way back from Colorado?"

Josh glared at Murphy and refused to answer.

Zach's ice blue gaze narrowed over his partner's taut features. "Something wrong, Josh?"

"No," Josh snapped.

"Of course there's somethin' wrong," Murphy declared. "He's been cranky as a bear, snarlin' and growlin' ever since I got here."

Before Josh could respond, or Zach ask another question, the door to the ranch house burst open and a little boy dashed out onto the porch.

Josh froze, his gaze narrowing as he stared at the

boy. Zach half turned, and Murphy glanced over his shoulder at the unexpected interruption.

The child jumped down the shallow steps and was halfway to the gate when a woman stepped onto the porch, pulling the door shut behind her.

"J.J.!"

Her voice carried clearly on the early-morning air. Josh registered the musical, feminine tones and a muscle jumped in his clenched jaw, a barely perceptible flinch jerking his big body.

"Don't go outside the fence."

"Hurry up, Mommy." The little boy climbed onto the bottom rung of the wooden gate and peered over the top, his eyes rounding as he spotted the men, trucks and horse in front of the barn. "Look, Mommy, a horse!"

Sarah glanced up from her ring of keys and across the intervening space between the ranch house and barn. Three men stood there. One of them was Murphy Redman, a white-haired, bowlegged neighboring rancher, while the second, a tall blond man, Sarah recognized as Zach Colby, a friend of Josh's.

The third man was Josh Hightower.

Chapter Two

"Mommy, can I go pet the horse? Can I?"

Sarah didn't know how long she'd been standing frozen, staring at Josh's rigid figure, before the repeated tugging on her arm brought her attention back to J.J.

"I'm sorry, honey, what did you say?"

"The horse—can I go see the horse?"

Impatiently he pointed across the yardlot to the barn, bouncing excitedly up and down.

"No, J.J. You can't." She ignored his quick frown and took his hand in hers. "Aunt Molly is expecting you, and I have to go to the hospital to see Grandma Patricia."

"I'd rather pet the horse," J.J. said stubbornly.

"Maybe Uncle Wes will take you out to see his horses," Sarah told him. She walked with him to the car, then pulled open the door and urged him firmly inside.

She refused to look toward the barn again, but she could feel the weight of Josh's unrelenting stare as she drove away from the house, the image of his broad shoulders and his long legs encased in faded tight jeans engraved on her memory.

The three men stood silently, watching the woman and little boy until the car disappeared down the lane and turned onto the highway.

Murphy whistled, the long, low expulsion of air a sound of disbelief. "If I'm not mistaken, that woman was Sarah Drummond."

Josh was silent. Murphy turned away from the now-empty lane and eyed him. "What's she doin' here, Josh?"

Josh didn't answer. A muscle ticked in his clenched jaw, his eyes burned with fury and his hands were curled into fists.

"The postmistress told me Patricia Drummond is in the hospital," Zach said when Josh didn't answer. "Maybe Sarah is back because her mother's sick."

"Umm," Murphy grunted in acknowledgment. "Makes sense, but that still doesn't explain what she's doin' *here*. Why's she stayin' in the house?"

"No reason why she can't," Zach said slowly. "It belongs to her."

"So what?" Murphy demanded. "You two leased this place."

"Not the house. We didn't need it, and I didn't want to be responsible if pipes froze or kids decided to break out windows in an empty house."

"Oh."

Josh was only half listening to the conversation. He'd thought he didn't care if she was married—until last night when she'd said "we." He'd wanted to put his fist through the nearest wall, just thinking about Sarah with another man. And now this morning, a little boy had run out of the house and called her "Mommy." Living, breathing proof that she belonged to someone else. Had a child with someone else. The sharp sense of betrayal that filled him at the thought of Sarah with another man didn't make sense, but that didn't make it any easier to live with.

He spun and stalked to his truck, yanking open the door.

"Josh!"

Murphy's yell stopped him, and he looked back over the hood of the pickup. The older man's face was worried. "What?" he asked impatiently.

"Where are you going?"

"To work. There's a line of fence down in the south pasture that needs new wire and posts." Josh didn't wait for a response. He slid into the truck and slammed the door. The engine growled obediently to life when he twisted the key, and he rammed the four-speed transmission into gear, gravel spitting from beneath the wheels as he left the yard.

Josh sat on his front porch, the wooden chair tipped onto its back legs. His hair was still wet from the shower, his long, jeans-clad legs stretched out in front of him, bare feet crossed at the ankles and propped on the top railing.

He'd shrugged into a shirt after his shower, but he hadn't bothered buttoning it, and the blue cotton fell open across his chest. An open bottle of Jack Daniel's sat on the washboard muscles of his midriff, his fingers curled around the neck.

He lifted the bottle and drank, grimacing briefly at the sharp bite of the amber liquid against his tongue before it slid smoothly down his throat. The whiskey hit his empty stomach and spread heat, warming him from the inside out.

He should eat something, he reflected morosely. He hadn't eaten anything all day and his stomach felt as if it was touching his backbone. But he didn't move. The only thing in the refrigerator was ham and eggs, and he didn't feel like cooking.

It was after ten o'clock. Behind him, the house was unlit and silent. Before him, the night was equally dark and equally quiet, except for the occasional chatter of quarreling raccoons in the grove of trees that partially blocked his view of the main house. He tilted the bottle again and stared unseeingly across the darkened land to the looming bulk of shadowy buttes.

Unrelenting hard work and the stoic, enduring land had sustained him and kept him sane when Sarah had left him five long years before. The long days spent beneath the burning summer sun and the demanding cold of winter, alone with his anger and grief amid the silent sweep of prairie and the towering buttes, had slowly healed his soul and brought him a kind of peace. Instinctively, he'd turned to hard labor this morning and had sought solitude in the pasture farthest from the ranch buildings in an attempt to deal with her return.

It hadn't worked. Alone with his thoughts, memories blindsided him and the pain of loss returned, accompanied by searing anger.

Five years ago he'd kissed her good-night at her door at midnight and she'd promised to meet him at Connie's Cafe at nine the following evening. He'd drunk untold cups of coffee and waited till closing time, but she never appeared. Her mother had stubbornly refused to tell him where Sarah had gone.

The pain of losing her had nearly cost him his sanity. It wasn't until nearly a year later that he heard from Sarah, in a letter that was brief and carefully polite. She told him that she had gotten on with her life and hoped that he had, too; she wished him well. She didn't tell him why she'd left, and to this day he didn't know where she'd gone or why.

I was over her, dammit. Why did she have to come back? The possibility that he hadn't learned to live without her, that he'd learned only to endure the loneliness her absence caused, nibbled at the edges of his consciousness, but he shoved it away.

Impatiently he surged to his feet, the chair falling back onto four legs with a thud.

"Hightower," he muttered aloud as he yanked open the screen door. "You're a fool. She's just another woman. Get over it."

With a decisive twist, he screwed the lid on the bottle and shoved it back in the cabinet where it belonged. He was damned if he was going to let Sarah Drummond drive him to drink.

Besides, he reflected derisively as he walked down the hallway to his bedroom, *alcohol isn't working.*

Sarah braced herself each time she and J.J. came and went from the Rocking D, silently praying that Josh would stay on his side of the grove of trees that separated the two houses. For several days it appeared as though he was avoiding her as carefully as she was him. She was glad, because each time she'd seen him, her hard-earned ability to deny her feelings and distance herself from emotion was shaken anew. She didn't need the distraction; she was having enough trouble dealing with her mother.

Patricia Drummond was a difficult woman to deal with when she was well. She was even more impossible when she was ill. Frustrated with her inability to speak and move about with the same agility she'd known before the stroke, she took her bad temper out on Sarah and the nurses.

Sarah knew from her consultation with the doctor that her mother's irascibility came more from her fear that she wouldn't recover than from actual pain. Still, sympathetic though Sarah was, Patricia's constant attacks left her feeling battered and exhausted.

On Saturday afternoon Patricia's bridge group crowded her hospital room, so Sarah escaped early, leaving her mother to enjoy the ongoing flow of gossip. J.J. was delighted when she picked him up from Molly's, and the moment they reached the Rocking D, he raced into the yard to play while Sarah found cold drinks.

With a glass of iced tea in one hand and apple juice in the other, she walked to the edge of the porch and scanned the front yard. "J.J., where are you?"

"I'm right here, Mommy."

His voice was accompanied by the creaky rasp of rope against wood and Sarah knew instantly where he was. The rope swing, tied to a sturdy limb on the big old box elder tree in the side yard, had made the same familiar sound when she was a child. Smiling fondly, she sat down on the wooden porch swing and watched J.J. as his legs pumped furiously to send the swing higher and higher toward the leafy umbrella above him.

"Careful, honey," she warned. "Don't go too high."

"Oh, Mom." The disgusted note in his voice told her in no uncertain terms what he thought of her warning. "I'm not a baby."

Sarah bit her tongue to keep from arguing with him. Being a single parent, she knew she tended to be overprotective, but sometimes J.J.'s need to assert his independence made her think he was hellbent on charging into danger.

The sound of an engine drew her attention away from J.J. She knew it couldn't be Josh; he'd been working with a horse in the corral connected to the barn when she and J.J. drove up, and he was still there. Try as she might, she couldn't ignore him; in fact, she was so sensitized to his presence that if it weren't physiologically impossible, she would swear that she had internal radar that went on alert anytime he was within a mile of her.

The dark blue pickup that pulled to a stop at her front gate had a Lazy H logo emblazoned on the driver's door. Sarah knew that the Lazy H ranch belonged to Josh and his brother, Lucas, but the young man driving the truck wasn't the least bit familiar to her. Curious, she pushed up out of the swing and walked to the porch steps, waiting while the passenger jumped out.

There was something vaguely familiar about the

slight young girl who rounded the hood of the truck and unlatched the gate. She had a backpack slung over one shoulder. Faded, ripped-at-the-knee jeans covered her legs, and an oversize white T-shirt was tucked into her waistband. She wore scuffed, high-top tennis shoes on her small feet and a worn denim jacket was tied around her waist by its sleeves. Her hair was glossy black and hung nearly to her waist in a braid as thick as a man's wrist. She couldn't have been more than eleven or twelve years old, but her small ears were quadruple pierced and sported silver studs and small hoops. But what really shocked Sarah was the multicolored bruise that surrounded her right eye.

"Hello," Sarah called when the girl was halfway up the path to the house. "Can I help you?"

The girl kept walking until she was only a few feet from the porch steps. She halted, stuck her hands into her back pockets and fixed Sarah with an intent stare. "I'm Caitlin Drummond," she said bluntly. "Are you my aunt Sarah?"

Sarah's mouth dropped open in surprise, and for a moment she was incapable of speech. "If you're Margaret's little girl, then yes, I'm your aunt Sarah," she finally managed to get out.

"I'm nobody's little girl," Caitlin responded flatly, her voice devoid of inflection. "But Margaret is my mother."

Sarah was nonplussed. The thin young girl's grass green eyes held far too much world-weary cynicism for her years. Fatigue had smudged dark circles under her eyes and her smooth, tanned skin was drawn taut over classic cheekbones. Sarah searched for other similarities between the young girl standing at the foot of the steps and her sister, Margaret.

"You look like her," Sarah said slowly. "Except for the hair and the eyes." Margaret was as fair as Sarah, and the sisters had both inherited their father's blue eyes. But the shape of Caitlin's face, the beautifully molded cheekbones and stubborn chin—those Margaret had passed on to her only child.

Caitlin shrugged. "Yeah, that's what she says."

J.J. jumped off the still-moving swing and came racing across the lawn. He stopped several feet away from Caitlin and surveyed her with bright, fascinated eyes.

"Who're you?" he asked.

"This is your cousin, Caitlin," Sarah told him. "She's come all the way from Los Angeles to visit—" Her words came to an abrupt halt. "How did you get here, Caitlin? Your mother didn't call and tell me that you were coming."

"She didn't know," Caitlin said. "I hitchhiked."

"You did what?" Sarah was aghast. "You're kidding me, right?" She heard the click of the pickup door, the crunch of boots against gravel, and knew that the driver was opening the gate. But she didn't glance up. All her attention was focused on her niece.

"I caught rides with long-haul truckers as far as Wolf Point, then Trey picked me up and brought me here."

"Did you get that black eye in an accident? Or from a trucker?" Sarah couldn't have been more angry if J.J. had been the one attacked. Every protective instinct she owned went on instant alert, and she could feel her cheeks heat. Her own brief but devastating experience with male violence had scarred her deeply; the possibility that Caitlin's face had been marked by a fist rather than an unnamed accident touched off an anger within Sarah that bordered on rage.

"Neither." Caitlin's green gaze turned wary, but she didn't back away from Sarah. "I'm not going back to L.A.," she said with force. "Not until Margaret gets a new boyfriend."

"Is that who hit you—the boyfriend?" Sarah asked swiftly, quick to pick up on the dislike in Caitlin's voice.

Caitlin refused to answer. She stood silently, staring stubbornly at Sarah.

"She wouldn't tell me, either."

Distracted by the male voice, Sarah's gaze lifted from Caitlin's closed face and for the first time she really looked at the driver of the pickup. Blond, blue-eyed and handsome, he was young, probably no more than twenty, and his tall, broad-shouldered frame gave promise of strength and power when he matured. Dressed in boots, jeans, a faded T-shirt and a straw cowboy hat, he stood a step behind Caitlin, backing her with silent support.

"I'm Trey Weber," he volunteered. "I work for Lucas Hightower. I picked up Caitlin just this side of Wolf Point."

"Thank you, Trey, it was kind of you to bring her all the way to me."

"No problem, I was coming over to help Josh do some work on the barn, anyway."

"Oh. I see." Sarah stiffened.

"I'm sure you don't remember me," he said casually. "I only went to work for Lucas about four or five years ago. I think you left Butte Creek before I moved here."

"Yes, I must have," Sarah replied. The young man was watching her closely, as if he were searching for a reaction, an expression—something. Sarah had no idea what he was looking for, only that his expectant, perceptive stare was disconcerting. "Well, Caitlin," she said with purposeful cheerfulness, "I'm sure you must be hungry and tired. Why don't we go inside and I'll make us all some lunch."

"All right." Caitlin took a step forward before halting and turning abruptly. "Thanks for the ride, Trey."

"Hey, no problem, kid." Trey grinned, white teeth flashing in his tanned face. He reached out and gently tugged the loose end of her braid. "Just don't go hitching any rides with strangers again, okay? Next time you might get some pervert instead of a nice guy like me."

Caitlin sniffed scornfully and pulled her braid forward over her shoulder and out of his hand. "Yeah, right."

He chuckled, a deep sound of amusement, and glanced at Sarah. "It was a pleasure meeting you, ma'am."

From the corral Josh had watched the interchange while grooming a young colt. He gave up all pretense of indifference, however, when Trey parked his truck outside the barn and climbed over the corral fence.

"Who's the girl?" he asked, his hands continuing the soothing, rhythmic movement of the brushes over the colt's glossy hide.

"Caitlin Drummond," Trey answered. "I picked her up just north of Wolf Point. She hitchhiked all the way from L.A. Can you believe any twelve-year-old kid taking a chance like that? Pretty gutsy."

"Not to mention stupid," Josh responded. "And dangerous."

"Yeah, you got that right." Trey took a brush from a box of grooming supplies leaning against the bottom corral pole and moved to the far side of the colt. "I hitched a few rides when I was younger, but never across that many miles.'' Silence reigned for a few moments. ''She's got a black eye that looks like it's a few days old. She wouldn't tell her aunt who gave it to her.''

Josh got a sharp, sick feeling in his stomach. ''One of her rides beat her up?''

''She told her aunt they didn't. Caitlin wouldn't admit it, but I suspect it was her mother's boyfriend in L.A. who popped her.''

''Margaret Drummond never did have any sense,'' Josh growled in disgust. ''It doesn't surprise me that she's seeing some guy who would hit a kid.''

''You know her?'' Trey asked with curiosity.

''Yeah, she was a year behind me in school.''

''No kiddin'? Did you ever date her?''

''No.'' *I dated her little sister.*

Again silence stretched, both men occupied with their own thoughts.

''They both have sad eyes,'' Trey said finally, almost to himself.

''Who does?'' Josh asked, bending to slide the brush down the colt's foreleg.

''Caitlin and her aunt Sarah.''

Josh jerked upright and stared across the colt's glossy back at Trey.

''Well, they do,'' Trey said when Josh continued to glare at him. ''Caitlin's got that 'I've seen it all and the world stinks' look in her eyes and a chip a yard wide on her shoulders. Her aunt's got the same look, only without the attitude.''

"Hmmph," Josh grunted, irritated. "Since when did you become a psychiatrist? Or maybe you're psychic? You don't even know them."

Trey shrugged. "I recognize the look. I've been there, remember? I used to see it in my mirror every morning when I was a kid."

Josh had a sudden, swift memory of the first time he'd met Trey, a too-thin fifteen-year-old with a lifetime of neglect behind him. The five years between then and now had made immense changes in Trey, but apparently it hadn't been long enough for him to forget what his life had been like.

"You may be right about the girl. Having Margaret for a mother can't be any fun. But Sarah had a father who doted on her and gave her everything his money could buy when she was growing up. Whatever you saw in her eyes, it wasn't put there by a world that kicked her in the teeth." Josh gave the colt's sleek back one last stroke of the brush and stepped back, tossing the brushes into the box behind him. He untied the colt and caught the lead just below the halter's chin strap. "As soon as I put Golden Boy back in his stall, we can get started on the roof."

Sarah glanced out her kitchen window just as the two men and the horse disappeared into the barn. Distracted by the gleam of hot sun in Josh's coal black hair and the slow, unconscious swagger in his walk, she stared out the window long after the corral was empty.

Behind her, J.J. chattered nonstop as he quizzed Caitlin about her trip and Los Angeles.

"Do you live at Disneyland?" he asked.

"No. Nobody lives at Disneyland," she answered. Tap water ran over her soapy hands and she bent to scrub her face in the kitchen sink.

"Uh-huh!" J.J. objected. Perched on his knees on a chair at the kitchen table, he propped his elbows on the table. "Mickey Mouse and Pluto live there."

Caitlin dried her face with a towel and gave him a long-suffering glance. "I meant real people. Real people don't live at Disneyland."

"Oh." He contemplated her shiny face for a moment. "You wanna see my swing?"

"Not until after lunch, J.J.," Sarah interrupted, dragging her thoughts away from Josh. "Then if Caitlin isn't too tired, you can show her the swing. She's been traveling for a long time and she might not feel like playing this afternoon."

"I don't mind," Caitlin told her quickly. "I'm good with little kids. I baby-sit all the time for the neighbors at home. I'll help you take care of J.J. while I'm here."

"All right," Sarah said calmly. Caitlin was clearly letting her know that she wouldn't be a liability.

Hours later, when both J.J. and Caitlin were tucked into beds upstairs, Sarah acknowledged that Caitlin was, indeed, good with kids. J.J. had followed her around chattering nonstop, obviously fascinated by the twelve-year-old's vast store of tough, worldly wisdom. For her part, Caitlin was amazingly patient with J.J.

Sarah located her sister's phone number and took time to brew a hot cup of tea before she dialed Margaret. Surprisingly, the receiver was picked up on the third ring.

"Yeah?"

The male voice that barked in her ear startled Sarah. "Hello, is this the Margaret Drummond residence?"

The phone clattered and Sarah heard the muted male voice as the man called her sister's name.

"Hello?"

"Margaret, this is Sarah."

"Sarah! Hi, what are you—" The surprise in Margaret's voice quickly shifted to concern. "Is it Mother? Is she worse?"

"No," Sarah responded quickly, reassuringly. "She's about the same, maybe a little better, although progress is slow." The telephone line carried Margaret's quick, soft sigh of relief. "I'm not calling about Mother, Margaret. It's Caitlin."

"What about Caitlin?" Margaret's voice sharpened. "Have you heard from her?"

"She's here. She got here this afternoon. She said she hitchhiked all the way from Los Angeles."

"That little idiot!" Margaret said impatiently. "I knew I'd hear from her sooner or later, but it never occurred to me that she'd go all the way to Montana!"

Sarah was speechless for a moment. It wasn't the response she'd been expecting. "Where did you think she was?" she finally asked.

"Oh, at one of her friends' houses. She does this every now and then, you know, just disappears for a few days when things don't go her way here at home."

"You mean she's done this before?"

"Heavens, yes." Margaret sounded put-upon. "She's always been a difficult child and the older she gets, the more difficult she becomes."

Sarah knew she and Margaret had never been close. Not only were they separated in age by seven years, but they were further set apart by their personalities. The fun-loving Margaret had teased her little sister, calling her Sober Sarah, when she bothered to notice her at all. Sarah hadn't seen her sister since Caitlin was a two-year-old; since then, their contact had been limited to infrequent phone calls when Margaret needed money. Even so, Margaret's seeming indifference to Caitlin's safety shocked Sarah.

"Actually, Sarah," Margaret continued, "I'm glad she's with you in Montana. It's the perfect place for her to spend the summer, and I don't want her back in L.A. for a while. The two of us really need breathing space away from each other. I have a new man in my life and Caitlin is being more difficult than usual. She's always been an exceptionally bright, impossible-to-control child.''

Margaret's voice held a cajoling note that Sarah remembered vividly. She'd heard it too many times as a child whenever Margaret wanted something.

"Caitlin has a black eye that looks like it's a few days old,'' she said, keeping her voice neutral. "Do you know how she got it?''

"Of course not!'' Margaret answered defensively. "How would I know? She must have got it after she left L.A., probably from somebody that gave her a ride.''

Sarah didn't bother asking her if the new boyfriend might have hit Caitlin. Even if Margaret knew he had, she'd probably deny the truth.

"So,'' Margaret continued brightly, "will you keep Caitlin? If you can't, then she can go to Aunt Molly's. I'm sure she and Wes would love to have some company for the summer.''

"She'll stay with me,'' Sarah said abruptly, disgusted with Margaret's callous disregard for Caitlin's feelings. "I have to go now. I'll call you if Mother's condition changes.''

She didn't wait for Margaret's response. She returned the receiver very carefully to its cradle, when what she wanted to do was slam it down.

Muttering to herself about the injustice of children being given to irresponsible, uncaring parents, she turned out the lights and went upstairs to bed.

Unfortunately for Sarah, Patricia's bridge group spent more time gossiping than they spent playing cards when they visited her at the hospital. Sarah barely had time to drop her purse and a florist's cone of blue and white daisies and pink carnations on the windowsill the next day before Patricia launched into a speech.

"Is it true that Josh Hightower is living in the foreman's house at the ranch?" she demanded angrily, struggling with the words.

Sarah's heart sank, but with a control gained painfully over the past several years, she managed not to reveal the dismay she felt. "Yes, Mama, he is."

"Then what are you doing there?"

"I can't afford to stay in a motel indefinitely, and your house in town isn't livable," Sarah said patiently.

"Then go to Wes and Molly's," Patricia ordered.

"I can't stay with them, Mama," Sarah replied evenly. "As much as I love Uncle Wes, I'm just not comfortable living in the house with him—or any male except J.J."

"Hmmph," Patricia snorted inelegantly. "I should think it would be easier to be in the same house with your uncle Wes than to be on the same property with that Hightower boy. It's positively indecent—you might as well be living together! People are going to talk.''

"We aren't living together. We're farther apart than if we lived down the block from each other in town. And no one would find anything wrong with that.''

Patricia glared at her, her lips compressed in a thin line. "Have you told him?'' she finally rapped out.

Sarah stiffened. "No, Mama, I haven't told him.''

"Well, thank heavens you've shown some sense. It's bad enough that I have to dodge questions about when you got married and where J.J.'s father is. I don't know what everyone would say if they knew the truth.''

"No, Mama,'' Sarah said wearily. "I don't know what any of your friends would say if they knew the truth, either. And even more to the point, I don't know what Josh would say.''

Silenced by the depth of desolation in her daughter's eyes, Patricia snapped her mouth shut on a caustic comment. She was uncharacteristically docile and cooperative for the rest of Sarah's visit.

Two days later Sarah, J.J. and Caitlin walked onto the front porch after dinner just as Josh approached.

Sarah halted at the porch railing while the children raced down the walkway to the gate. She'd seen Josh ride by the house several times over the past week; he'd never bothered looking her way, and she assumed the pattern would be repeated.

J.J. and Caitlin, however, had other plans.

"Hey, mister!" J.J.'s clear treble carried easily on the warm, early-evening air. "Hey, mister! Can we pet your dog?"

Sarah shaded her eyes with one hand. She'd been so focused on Josh that she hadn't really noticed the bay quarter horse he rode, nor the huge black Labrador dog that loped alongside him.

Caitlin lifted the latch and the two children shoved open the gate and ran toward the dog and horse.

"J.J.! Caitlin! Come back here!" Sarah left the safety of the porch and hurried down the walk to the gate.

The big dog swung his head toward the children and barked, a deep, inquiring woof of sound, and veered away from the horse.

Sarah's heart lodged in her throat. The dog was so big that his huge head was level with J.J.'s face.

"J.J.!"

"Rum!" Josh's deep voice growled the name, and the dog halted immediately. Still, his tail wagged steadily, his body quivering as he stretched his nose forward as far as he could toward the nearing children. "Down."

Rum stretched out on the ground, pink tongue

lolling, brown eyes alight with interest as J.J. and Caitlin reached him. They eyed the dog with equal interest.

"Does he bite?" Caitlin asked.

Saddle leather creaked, the bit jingling as Josh dismounted in one easy motion. "No, he doesn't bite. You can pet him if you want."

Josh pretended to ignore Sarah's tense figure, but he knew she gripped the gate and watched the children with his big dog. He damned the curiosity that had made him rein in and stop; for the past week he'd watched Sarah come and go with the children and waited for a glimpse of her husband. There hadn't been one. Slowly it had occurred to him that maybe the "he" she'd referred to that first day had been her son.

He went down on his heels next to Rum and laid a hand on his collar. Reassured, the children came closer, laughing when Rum's tongue swiped them with friendly wetness when they ventured to pat his head.

"Gosh, he's sure big, mister," J.J. said, eyeing Rum's big paws with awe.

"He is that," Josh agreed, unable to suppress a small grin at the amazement in the little boy's green eyes. He listened to the children exclaim over Rum's impressive size while he watched J.J. Something about the little boy wasn't quite right, and he couldn't put his finger on what it was that nagged him. He'd only seen the kid from a distance; up close, he realized that the child was taller than he'd thought, and the lively intelligence on his face made him seem older. There was something hauntingly familiar about the boy's thick-lashed emerald eyes and the way they crinkled at the corners when he laughed at Rum. But Josh was positive he'd never known anyone with eyes that brilliant shade of green.

"How old is he?" Caitlin asked, stroking Rum's deep black pelt with appreciation.

"Only two," Josh replied.

"I'm older than him," J.J. said importantly, his own small hand smoothing over Rum's ear. "I'm four."

Josh went completely still. *Four?*

"No kidding," he replied, his voice nearly expressionless. "When's your birthday?"

"Just before Christmas." J.J.'s eyes sparkled. "Mommy says I'm the best present she ever got."

Josh didn't answer. He couldn't answer. His glance shot from the little boy's face to Sarah. She stood frozen, her face pale. She'd clearly heard every word they'd said, and she looked guilty as hell.

"Can he play with us in the yard?" Caitlin asked.

Josh tore his gaze away from Sarah and looked back at the children. They were watching him with hopeful, expectant faces.

"Yeah," he said rustily, and cleared his throat. "Yeah, he can go play in the yard with you."

He released Rum's collar and stood. The children and dog surged to their feet, racing back through the gate, past a motionless Sarah, and disappeared around the corner of the house.

Josh forced his body to move, but he didn't speak until he was only a few feet from her. He stopped and stared at her. Pale but composed, she watched him, her slim body taut and still.

"He's four years old?"

Sarah nodded but didn't speak.

Shock was giving way to incredulous acceptance, followed swiftly by a bright flame of anger.

"And you never told me? Four years and you never told me I had a son?"

Sarah flinched at his angry demand as if she'd taken a body blow. She'd hoped against hope that they would never have to have this conversation, prayed that somehow God would spare her this. Hadn't she suffered enough?

"I'm not sure you do have a son, Joshua."

"What does that mean?" He bit out the words. "If he's four years old and he was born around Christmas, then he's mine."

"I'm not sure that you're the father," Sarah said.

Stunned, Josh felt as if she'd hit him in the chest with a two-by-four. He could barely breathe.

"Are you telling me that you were sleeping with

someone else when we were together?'' he finally managed to ask her.

"Mommy!" J.J. raced around the corner of the house, followed by Rum and Caitlin. Unaware of the emotional drama he was interrupting, he tugged on Sarah's arm. "Rum's hungry. Can we give him a bone?"

Sarah tore her gaze away from Josh's face and the raw emotion written there. "You'll have to ask Mr. Hightower, J.J. You mustn't feed someone else's pet."

"Can we, Mr. Hightower? Can we give him a bone?"

"Sure," Josh said carefully. He felt as if a crevasse had opened below his feet and he teetered on the crumbling edge.

The children ran to the porch and disappeared into the house.

"Josh, I—"

"Mommy, can Rum have the roast left from dinner?" They were back, the three of them crowded into the doorway, the screen pushed open.

Sarah sighed with frustration. "I'll come find him something." She turned back to Josh, lowering her voice. "I know we need to talk about this, Joshua, but I'd rather do it when the children aren't around, especially J.J. Will you wait until I put them to bed?"

He wanted to say no. Every cell in his body demanded that she answer his questions now, but one glance behind her at J.J., hopping from one foot to the other in the doorway, told him there was no way they could have this conversation without interruption.

"All right. What time?"

"Nine o'clock. They should both be asleep by then."

"All right. I'll be back at nine. And you'd better be ready to talk," he said grimly.

Sarah watched wordlessly as he turned away from her and stalked to his horse. He never looked back at her as he swung lithely aboard and rode off toward the barn.

She almost wished that she could have told him yes. Yes, she'd been having an affair with another man while they'd been together. But it was a lie.

And the truth was worse. So much worse that she'd decided long ago that she was never going to tell him everything.

Chapter Three

Sarah's hands were shaking so badly that she smeared her lipstick. Impatiently, she took a tissue and wiped her lips, carefully concentrating on holding her hand steady as she reapplied the pink color.

The reflection in the mirror showed her a woman with pale cheeks and haunted eyes. She dusted blusher across her cheeks and brushed her lashes with mascara, then eyed herself critically in the bathroom mirror. The makeup wasn't to impress Josh; it was for her own protection. One of the things she'd learned about herself was that makeup and clothing became a disguise that created the illusion of self-confidence and calmness. Few people were observant enough to look beyond the surface image.

To face Josh she needed all the assistance she could get. Her hair needed only a quick brushing to restore its customary sleekness, and Sarah gave her clothes a quick, inspecting glance. She still wore the sandals, tan linen shorts and cream-colored silk T-shirt that she'd worn to the hospital that morning. Small gold hoops gleamed at her ear-lobes and she wore a slim wristwatch on her left wrist. She glanced at the crystal face and drew a deep breath. It was five minutes to nine.

Knuckles rapped on the front door just as she reached the bottom step of the stairs. Sarah froze and drew another steadying deep breath before crossing the entryway to pull open the door.

Josh didn't say anything. For one long, silent moment they stood motionless, staring at each other through the screen door before Sarah pushed it open.

"Come in." Sarah was already turning away as he caught the edge of the door and stepped through. "Let's go into the kitchen," she said.

He followed her across the entryway and down the shadowy hall.

"Sit down, Josh." Aware of his broad bulk behind her, she moved quickly past the table to the counter. Her back to him, she poured coffee into two mugs and turned, only to halt abruptly. He hadn't taken a seat at the table. He was still standing, his unreadable gaze fastened on her. He'd changed into clean jeans and shirt, his jaw freshly shaven and his black hair still shower-wet.

She held out one of the mugs. "Coffee?"

He took it from her and set it down on the counter with a controlled violence that sent the black liquid sloshing over the rim. "I didn't come here for coffee, Sarah. Talk to me. Is J.J. mine or isn't he?"

Sarah took a deep breath, struggling to control the shaking that started deep inside and sent waves of reaction outward. Her fingers trembled where they gripped the mug, but she forced herself to meet his gaze calmly.

"I don't know, Josh." She saw the impatience and fury that flared in his eyes, but she kept speaking. "He might be, or he might have been fathered by another man, but even if—"

"Who?" Josh growled.

Sarah drew a deep breath. Anger radiated from his big body, and the air between them was thick with tension. "I'm not going to tell you, Josh."

"Why not? I think I have a right to know who else you were sleeping with while you were lying and telling me I was the only one."

The barb struck home; Sarah flinched from the pain. "I refuse to argue with you over this, Josh. What's done is done."

Josh felt like hitting something. Anything. Unfortunately, the only other person in the room was Sarah, and furious though he was, she looked pale and fragile. Besides, he'd never hit a woman in his life.

"Did you tell him that he might have given you a child?"

The little color remaining in Sarah's face disappeared entirely.

"No," she said evenly. "I never told him."

"So you decided that you wouldn't tell either of us. Didn't you think we had a right to know?"

"No." Her response was swift. "I didn't."

Frustrated at her short, uninformative replies, Josh paced away from her, pausing at the window before turning to face her. "Why not?"

"I never told you, Josh, because I knew very well that you had no interest at all in being a father. In fact, you hated the very idea."

"What? Where did you get that idea?"

"From you," Sarah replied promptly. "I can't count the number of times when we were dating that you told me you were never getting married and never having children. You were absolutely adamant about your feelings."

"That's not true," Josh denied.

"I didn't imagine those conversations, Josh." Sarah didn't add that every one of them was engraved on her memory. How foolish she'd been, and how young, for she'd hoped that she would change his mind. Fate hadn't given her the time to try.

Josh stared at her. Was it true? Five years ago

he'd been younger, more bitter about his parents and their destructive impact on his life. He'd agreed with his older brother, Lucas, that marriage was a hell he never wanted for himself. And kids?

He thrust his fingers through his hair in an unconscious gesture of frustration. "Hell, maybe you're right, maybe I did tell you that. I said a lot of stupid things when I was younger. That doesn't mean I wouldn't have taken care of the problem if I'd gotten you pregnant."

Sarah stiffened. "J.J. isn't a *problem,* Josh. He's a little boy. And neither of us are a problem that you need to take care of. We take care of ourselves just fine!"

"That's not what I meant, and you know it, Sarah," Josh growled. She clearly hadn't wanted an offer of marriage from him. *Marriage.* The word slammed into his brain and he tensed. "Did you marry him?"

Sarah didn't pretend that she didn't understand what Josh meant. "No," she said, unable to keep the loathing from her voice. "I've never been married."

Josh picked up on the undertones in her voice, but couldn't quite decipher what they meant. "Whose name did you put on J.J.'s birth certificate?"

"No one's. I listed his father as 'unknown.'"

Josh bit off a curse and glared at her. "You told the whole world that he's illegitimate? Couldn't you at least have had the decency to name a father?''

"I know that I'm his mother and that he's my son. That's all I need to know."

"Maybe that's all *you* need to know, but it sure as hell isn't all *I* need to know. I want to have blood tests done to find out if he's mine."

"No!" Panic gripped Sarah. "I don't want J.J. tested."

"Why not?" Josh stared at her. Her eyes were dark in a face pale with stress. She was gripping her mug so tightly that her knuckles were white, and a fine tremor shivered the surface of the coffee.

"I just don't want to put J.J. through tests," she said evasively. "I don't want him upset. Isn't it enough that he has your name?"

"He has my name? I thought you said you listed his father as unknown?"

"I did," Sarah answered quickly. "But his given name is Joshua Jonathon Drummond. I named him after you and my father."

"Damn you, Sarah," Josh said softly, his voice lethal with suppressed fury. "I want to know if he's really mine. I want our blood tested."

"No."

"I'm not asking you anymore, Sarah, I'm telling you. If you won't agree, I'll see my attorney and ask him to do whatever it takes to get a court order to force you to cooperate."

Sarah stared at him without flinching. It took

every bit of courage she owned to face the towering anger that blazed in his eyes. "Please, Josh, don't do this. I can't—"

"You can. Why are you making such a federal case out of this? It's not as if drawing blood from J.J. will hurt him." She didn't answer and he bit off a curse. "Think about it, Sarah. I won't wait forever." He turned and stalked from the room.

Sarah stood, frozen in place, until she heard the front door close with a quiet slap that more sharply revealed his anger than if he'd slammed it.

It wasn't until she heard the measured tread of his boots across the porch boards and the ensuing silence that followed that she slumped. Muscles quivering with reaction, she managed to walk the short distance to the table and drop into a chair. The hard-won control that had kept her spine stiff deserted her, and she stared unseeingly at the empty doorway, devastated at his response.

She'd always known Josh would hate her when she told him that J.J.'s father might be another man. She'd always known that he would believe that she had betrayed him on the most basic level, because she couldn't bring herself to say the words that would prove differently. That she had been so far off the mark about his reaction to the possibility of fatherhood was unexpected and unacceptable. She struggled to equate his reaction tonight with the man who had told her five years earlier that he never wanted to have children.

For five years she had stubbornly clung to the belief that making love with Josh had created the son she loved so fiercely. She'd always known that blood tests could prove the identity of J.J.'s biological father beyond any doubt. Ever since his birth, she'd agonized over whether to initiate testing. Through long, sleepless nights she'd struggled to evenly weigh Josh and J.J.'s needs and their right to know the truth with her own deep-seated fear. She loved Josh. On some deep, primal level, the possibility that anyone but Josh could have fathered the son she loved so fiercely wounded her to the soul and threatened her sanity.

Still, her deeply ingrained sense of fairness told her that she owed Josh the cooperation that would answer his question about her son's father. Yet how would she survive emotionally if tests proved that Josh wasn't J.J.'s father?

How would she deal with Josh if the tests proved that he *was* J.J.'s father?

Three days later a nervous mare balked at being loaded into a horse trailer and lashed out, clipping Murphy Redman with a shod hoof and snapping his lower leg bone.

Josh had taken the crotchety rancher to the emergency room. Now Murphy rested in a hospital room that smelled of antiseptic and gleamed with shiny white and chrome surfaces. Josh watched the nurse tuck a sheet and light blanket over Murphy's shoulders before she stepped away from the bed.

"He'll be groggy from the medication for the rest of the day." She smiled at Josh, her blue eyes kind in a face lined with experience and time. "The doctor left a prescription if he has pain during the night. You're welcome to stay if you want, but he's going to be sleeping and probably won't know that you're here."

Josh eyed the thick cast covering the old horseman's leg and sighed, scrubbing a hand wearily over his face.

"I'll stay a few minutes and then go on home. You'll call me if he needs anything?"

"Of course."

She left the room, the door whooshing quietly shut behind her.

Josh walked to the bed. Murphy's eyes were closed, his white hair mussed against the pillow, his face pale. His lanky body seemed smaller beneath the white sheets, the vital energy that was so much a part of him muted.

"Murphy?" Josh whispered, gently clasping his hand over the older man's wrist.

Murphy's eyelids fluttered in a small movement of response, but he didn't waken. Josh squeezed his arm gently and stepped back from the bed. With one last assessing glance, he turned and walked quietly to the door, pausing to switch off the light. To his surprise, the room was thrown into semidark-

ness, the only light in the room the soft glow of a
night-light near the bed and moonlight that shafted
through the window. It had been late afternoon
when he'd reached the hospital with Murphy, and
night had fallen while he'd waited for the older man
to be X-rayed and have his leg set and casted.

Josh stepped out into the hall, settled his hat over
his forehead and turned to leave. He stopped in
midstride. Two doors down, Sarah Drummond
leaned her forehead and clenched fists against the
white-enameled wall, tears streaming down her
face. Beneath the soft yellow cotton of her sundress,
her shoulders moved with silent, tearing sobs and
Josh stiffened under the rush of fierce emotion that
gripped him.

He stood motionless while he battled the need to
stride down the hall and pull her into his arms to
comfort her and the equally strong, sure knowledge
that he should turn his back and walk away.

Before he could do either, a white-coated doctor
brushed past him. The man's crepe-soled shoes
made no noise on the polished hall floor and when
he paused behind Sarah, she continued to cry silently, eyes closed, clearly unaware that he was
there. The man glanced over his shoulder at Josh
and lifted an eyebrow, but when Josh didn't respond, he turned back to Sarah.

The doctor reached out, one hand gently closing
over the curve of Sarah's shoulder. "Ma'am, are
you all—"

Sarah spun to face him, arms lifted protectively.

Josh sucked in a breath. Her eyes were wide, filled with terror, her body tense and defensive.

The doctor instantly backed away and lifted his arms, his hands palm outward in a calming gesture of apology. "Sorry, ma'am, I didn't mean to scare you."

Sarah continued to stare at him for long moments while she visibly fought for control. At last the terror faded from her eyes and was slowly replaced by awareness and embarrassment. She slumped against the wall and lowered her arms to her sides, but her hands remained closed in tight fists.

"That's all right—I overreacted." Her voice trembled, the rush of adrenaline ebbing to leave her legs shaking and her heart hammering in her chest.

"Are you sure you're all right? Can I get you anything?"

"No, nothing, thank you—I'm fine." She gave him a shaky smile. "I didn't know you were there. You startled me."

The doctor stared at her for a moment before nodding and moving off down the hall.

It wasn't until the doctor disappeared around a corner that she drew a deep breath, glanced down the hall in the opposite direction…and saw Josh. Dressed in jeans, boots, shirt and hat, his clothing dusty and stained as if he'd just come in from work, he stood perfectly still, watching her with an unwavering stare that was disconcerting.

"Josh?" She paused and drew a deep breath, quickly blotting her wet cheeks and eyelashes with an already damp tissue before she pushed away from the wall and faced him. "What are you doing here?"

Josh moved at last, his steps slow and measured as he walked toward her. Her face was pale and bare of makeup, her eyelashes damp spikes surrounding eyes drenched with tears. He kept his hands tucked in his jean pockets, restraining the need to reach for her, while his brain tried to make sense of what he'd just seen. Sarah hadn't been startled—she'd been terrified; remnants of that terror still lurked in the depths of her eyes. What was going on?

"Murphy had an accident this afternoon. Broke his leg," he said, purposely choosing a safe, neutral subject. "He's just down the hall."

Sarah's eyes widened in surprise and concern. "I'm so sorry. Will he be all right?"

Josh nodded. "The doctor says he'll be in the cast for a while, but the break was clean and he's healthy and strong. In six months he'll be trying to ride every greenbroke horse on the place, just like he always has."

"Good." Sarah's relief was heartfelt. The old rancher had always been kind to her as a child, treating her and Margaret to cherry lollipops from his coat pocket when he visited her father. But after Jonathon Drummond's death, Patricia had moved her daughters to town, and Sarah had seldom seen Murphy after that.

Silence stretched. Josh nodded his head at the closed door just beyond Sarah's shoulder. "I heard your mother was ill. Is this her room?"

Sarah's lashes lowered, concealing her eyes, but not before he caught the flash of stark pain in the blue depths.

"Yes," she replied, her voice husky with emotion. "She...she had a stroke."

"Has something happened?" he prodded when she didn't go on. "Is her condition worse?"

Sarah shook her head. "No. In fact, the doctor told me today that she's progressing better than he had hoped."

"Then why are you crying?" he asked bluntly.

"No particular reason," she said evasively, reluctant to talk about her mother. "It's been a long day and I'm tired."

Josh lifted an eyebrow, disbelief coloring his voice. "And that made you cry?" She nodded silently, her glance avoiding his. "Hmm," he said noncommittally. He didn't believe her. He remembered vividly how difficult Sarah's relationship with her mother had been in the past and he doubted that time had softened Patricia Drummond. He also remembered how reluctant Sarah had been to discuss her mother five years ago, and how cleansing it had been for her when he'd coaxed her into confiding in him.

Irritated that he couldn't bring himself to simply ignore her tears, say good-night and go home, he stared at her for a long, charged moment. Finally, reluctantly, she met his gaze. The barely concealed distress he read there decided him.

"I missed dinner," he said abruptly. "Walk down to the cafeteria with me. I'll buy you a cup of coffee."

The invitation caught Sarah by surprise. He'd been furious with her three days ago. The last thing she'd expected was that he'd purposely seek her company.

"Come on, Sarah." A brief, self-derisive smile eased the stern lines of his face. "I promise I won't bite, or put arsenic in your coffee while your back's turned."

His smile destroyed the refusal she was about to utter. It had been so long since she'd seen him smile.

"All right." A responsive, brief smile lifted the downward curve of her mouth. "I have to collect my purse."

She disappeared into the room and Josh waited, silently berating himself for breaking his vow to stay far away from her.

They rode the elevator down to the main floor and traversed the short hallway to the cafeteria in silence. Josh ignored her protest that she wasn't hungry and ordered a bowl of thick vegetable soup and a turkey sandwich for each of them.

"Did you eat dinner?" he asked when she objected.

"No, not yet," she admitted. "But I'm not hungry."

Josh carried the tray across the nearly deserted, brightly lit cafeteria and slid it onto a table against the far wall. Sarah joined him, slipping into a chair, and glanced up when he set one of the bowls of soup in front of her.

"Just eat," he said before she could protest. "If you don't want more than a few bites, fine, but at least try. You look like a soft breeze would blow you away."

"I must look awful. I've been at the hospital since nine this morning." Sarah smoothed a hand self-consciously over her hair and reached for her purse. "I'm sure I don't have any lipstick on or..."

Josh reached out and gently clasped her wrist. She froze at the contact, her eyes going dark.

"Leave it. You look fine." Her skin was soft and warm under his hand, her pulse fast beneath his fingertips. He realized his thumb was stroking slowly against the delicate skin of her inner wrist and abruptly he released her. "All I meant was that you look tired—and hungry—so eat your soup."

Sarah drew a deep breath and picked up her spoon. It had surprised her when he reached out and caught her wrist in his hand, but she hadn't been suffocated with the usual blind panic.

Josh waited until her bowl was half-empty before he chose a neutral subject.

"Trey tells me that the girl staying with you is Margaret's daughter."

"Caitlin? Yes, she is." Sarah smiled.

"She doesn't look much like Margaret," he commented, noting that the lines of tension bracketing her soft mouth eased with the fond smile.

"No," Sarah agreed. "She has her father's black hair and green eyes, but her cheekbones and the shape of her face are carbon copies of Margaret's."

"Hmm," Josh compared his memory of Sarah's sister with the young girl he'd seen at the ranch and nodded in agreement. "That's some black eye she's got. Who's she been fighting with?"

Sarah's fingers tightened briefly over a pack of saltine crackers before she tore the cellophane open with unnecessary force. "She won't tell me, but I suspect it was Margaret's new boyfriend," she said grimly.

Josh bit off a curse of disgust. "Margaret needs to get a better class of friends if she's dating men who hit little girls," he growled.

"Exactly," Sarah answered emphatically. "I agree completely. Caitlin's going to spend the summer with me, and with any luck Margaret will have moved on to someone else by September."

"Even if she does, what are the odds that the next guy will be any better than this one?"

Sarah had been struggling with that very question

ever since her conversation with Margaret. "Not very good." She crumbled a cracker into her soup and looked up at him. "That's why I'm considering trying to keep Caitlin with me."

Josh's gaze narrowed over her. "Here? On the ranch?"

"Here, until Mama is back on her feet. Then Caitlin can go back to Great Falls with us."

Josh's spoon was halfway to his mouth when he paused and carefully lowered it, the soup untasted, back to the bowl. "Back to Great Falls? You're not staying here?"

"No. I took an emergency leave of absence from my job for three months, but I don't think I can be away any longer."

Josh forced himself to sip his coffee casually before speaking. "So, what is it you do in Great Falls?"

"I'm a public relations assistant at the Charles Russell Museum."

"A museum?" Josh remembered the trip he'd taken to Great Falls a few months after she'd disappeared from his life. A friend had insisted he'd seen Sarah in town, but Josh hadn't found her. *I never thought to look at the museum.* "Does that mean you get to make use of your talent for drawing?"

Sarah shook her head ruefully. "No, I'm afraid not. I spend more time organizing tours for schoolchildren than I spend sketching, but I love the kids and I enjoy the work.''

"How does your mother feel about what you're doing?'' Pretending to be completely absorbed in crumbling crackers into his remaining soup, Josh watched her through lowered lashes. He didn't miss the shadow of pain that moved swiftly across her face, instantly sobering her features.

"Mama isn't wholly satisfied with my choice of career.'' She framed the sentence carefully, softening her mother's critical view of her life.

"That sounds like a polite way of saying that she hates it,'' Josh said abruptly.

Startled, Sarah looked up at him. His blue eyes were shrewd and assessing; she hadn't fooled him a bit. He obviously hadn't forgotten that Patricia Drummond could be, and often was, a difficult woman. Sarah cradled her coffee mug in her hands and gave him a wry smile. "I can see I don't need to pretend with you, Josh.''

"I take it that your mother hasn't mellowed over the years,'' he commented dryly.

Sarah sighed. "No. I'd hoped that her illness would soften her, perhaps make her consider the choices I've made in my life under a different light. But Mama still disapproves of everything, from my clothes and my hair to my life-style.''

Josh skimmed a glance over the smooth, chin-length fall of silvery hair and what he could see above the table of her slim, curvy shape covered with the yellow sundress. "Well, I can tell she's clearly wrong about the clothes and hair. What is it she doesn't like about your life-style?"

An unexpected shiver of sexual awareness blind-sided Sarah when his gaze traveled from her face to her midriff and back again. Stunned, she stared at him, but decided that she'd imagined the brush of heat from his glance. His blue eyes held only impersonal inquiry when his gaze returned to meet hers.

"Mama thinks a woman who isn't married is a failure. She won't accept that I'm content with my job and J.J. She thinks my weekly schedule is atrocious."

"Why?" Josh kept his voice mild and a scowl from his face only with effort. He wanted her to keep talking, but his muscles tensed while he waited for her reply.

"Because I don't make time for any of the women's clubs where she has statewide memberships. J.J. and I participate in a Junior Rangers patrol at our neighborhood park and I volunteer as many hours as I can at his preschool. Between those activities and my five days a week at the museum, plus sitting on the committee that connects local schools and the museum, I barely have time to clean house and do the laundry after church on Sunday before it's Monday and time to start all over again." Sarah shook her head. "Mama just doesn't understand."

"It sounds like you work all the time."

"Not at all," she said quickly. "I like my job, and the hours I spend with J.J. or volunteering aren't work—they're really my play time."

"Hmm," Josh acceded. The brief comments she made about her life in Great Falls painted a picture of days filled with her son and work. The lack of a social life was glaringly obvious, and Josh wasn't sure if he liked the staggering relief that hit him to learn that she wasn't involved with anyone. Unfortunately for his peace of mind, he remembered all too well just exactly how involved she'd been with him five years before. Her passionate, uninhibited responses had driven him crazy, and the memories she'd left behind when she disappeared were indelible. Determined as he'd been to wipe her out of his mind with other women, he'd given up after the second disappointing encounter. It didn't seem to matter how beautiful and willing the women; they paled before the memory of Sarah.

Now the innocent, laughing, passionate girl he'd known had been replaced by a woman who carried herself with a strength and dignity that hid all but brief flashes of vulnerability.

He dragged his thoughts back to their conversation. "It still sounds like more work than play."

"Now you sound like my mother," Sarah chided him gently, smiling as he snorted in disgust.

"Not hardly." His lips quirked upward at the

sparkle of amusement that lit her eyes. "What does your mother think of Caitlin?"

"She hasn't seen her yet, but I don't doubt for a minute that Mama will be horrified by the pierced ears and ripped jeans. And Caitlin has the vocabulary of a Singapore dockhand. If she forgets herself and uses even one of her more colorful words, Mama will have a fit."

"That I can believe. Why haven't you taken her to visit her grandmother?"

"I haven't taken either of the kids to the hospital. I'm waiting until Mama's stronger. I don't think she is ready to deal with Caitlin, and J.J.'s so full of energy that he sometimes exhausts even me." *Not to mention that I'm sure Mama is reluctant to explain his existence to her friends.*

Across from her, Josh stiffened as if she'd slapped him, his features going hard and cold at the sound of Sarah's husky voice uttering the little boy's name. Listening to her, watching her, had almost made him forget the issue that lay like a gulf between them.

"Have you decided if you're going to let J.J. have his blood tested with me?" His voice was harsh, laced with irritation at the softening effect her distress had had on his anger.

Sarah flinched, and the half smile on her face disappeared. "No, I haven't," she admitted.

"Why not?" he demanded.

"It's not something I want done. There are a lot

of factors to consider and it's not a decision I can make overnight,'' she said carefully.

"I don't know why not," he retorted. "The decision seems pretty straightforward to me. Either you're going to cooperate or you're not."

"It's more complicated than that," Sarah insisted. "For one thing, the kind of tests you're talking about aren't done at a local doctor's office. They require a lab with special capabilities."

"So where do we need to go?"

"I'm not sure. But I know the tests can't be done locally."

"Then I'll fly us wherever it is we need to go to have them done. Great Falls? Missoula? Seattle?"

"I'm not sure. But I can't leave Butte Creek now. I came here to be with Mama. I can't leave until she's recovered."

"How long will that be?" he demanded, frustration evident in every tense line of his body.

"I don't know. Her doctor says she's doing as well as can be expected, but he's not able to predict how long before she can go home. She'll be moved from the hospital to a nursing home and will need physical therapy to regain as much movement as possible in her left side."

Josh ran his fingers through his hair, ruffling the black strands. "And he can't give you any kind of time frame?"

"No."

"Did he give you any indication as to how long it will be before he knows?"

"No." She shook her head. "I asked him just yesterday if he could make an educated guess as to when she can be moved to the nursing home. He told me that he's reviewing her case day by day. As soon as he's confident that her arrhythmia is under control, he'll have her moved, but he can't give us a definite date."

A muscle flexed in his jaw, and his eyes narrowed.

"I understand that you need to be close to the hospital in case there's a change in her condition, but you can at least decide whether or not you're going to cooperate with testing when your mother is well enough for you to be away for a day or two. I'm running out of patience, Sarah, and you're running out of time."

"I don't respond well to threats, Joshua." Sarah's gaze met his without flinching.

"I'm not threatening you, Sarah," he responded grimly. The burning need to know if J.J. was his son was a driving force. He'd already missed out on four years of the little boy's life. He didn't want to waste a single day more. "I'm stating a fact. Between your mother's illness and taking on Caitlin, I know you've got a lot to deal with at the moment, but you're being unreasonable about allowing blood tests of J.J., and I won't agree to let you put this off forever."

He shoved back his chair and stood, slapping his hat back on his head before stalking across the room to empty his tray.

Sarah sat still for a moment before she followed suit. To her surprise, he was waiting for her outside the cafeteria door. She paused, eyeing him warily.

"I'll follow you back to the ranch," he said shortly, answering the question in her glance. "It's late."

She nodded silently and walked beside him out to the parking lot, each carefully maintaining their distance. He waited until she'd unlocked the car door and slid inside before striding off to his truck. The reflection of his headlights in her rearview mirror were a constant reminder of his presence over each one of the thirty miles to the Rocking D.

Josh drove past without stopping when she parked in front of the ranch house; by the time she'd climbed the steps and crossed her porch, the sound of his truck engine had ceased. Sarah paused with her hand on the doorknob, and glanced over her shoulder just in time to see the lights flick on in the foreman's house.

It was disconcerting to have him living so near. Miles away from him in Great Falls, she'd been cocooned from life, any awareness of her sexuality frozen beneath layers of thick ice. She'd been convinced that her ability to react to any male had been cauterized and destroyed; yet being within sight and

sound of Josh had turned a blowtorch on her frozen
emotions. The thawing out was painful.

And much too late, she reflected. For even if a
miracle happened and she could bear being touched
by a man, Josh hated her.

She sighed wearily and pulled open the door. Inside, the house was quiet, only the faint sound of
voices and canned laughter from the television set
disturbing the peaceful stillness.

"Sarah? Is that you?"

"Yes, Aunt Molly." Sarah dropped her purse
and keys on the tiny hall table just as Molly Hildebrandt appeared in the living-room doorway. She
was a handsome woman, with long legs and a body
given more to lean grace than opulent curves, and
a warm, loving nature.

Beneath her short-cropped silver curls, her blue
eyes were filled with concern. "You look exhausted, child."

"I am," Sarah agreed. "It's been a long day."

"Come on back to the kitchen. I've got the kettle
on and we'll brew you a cup of tea." Molly caught
Sarah by the elbow and gently herded her down the
hall. "Have you eaten anything today?"

"Yes, I had a sandwich and soup."

"At the hospital cafeteria?" Molly sniffed when
Sarah nodded. "Assembly-line food! You may as
well try to chew cardboard."

They entered the kitchen and Molly shooed Sarah

into a chair at the table while she bustled around the old-fashioned kitchen.

"I was telling Wes just before you called today that I thought you seemed slimmer since you've been here. Are you losing weight?"

"Maybe a couple of pounds," Sarah admitted.

"You're doing too much. Margaret should be here to help—although to tell you the truth, Caitlin is probably more help than her mother would be. That girl is certainly good at entertaining J.J. He follows her around like a little puppy."

Sarah propped her chin on one hand and listened to Molly chatter. She'd missed her aunt during the years she'd spent in Great Falls, and only now realized how great a comfort the older woman had always been.

"...did the doctor say?"

Molly set a squat, rose-patterned teapot and two cups on the table and turned to retrieve a plate of thick molasses cookies from the counter.

"I'm sorry," Sarah said as she poured tea while Molly pulled out a chair and sat. "My mind wandered. What was the question?"

"What kept you at the hospital so late—did Patricia have a bad day?"

"Yes." Sarah closed her eyes and gently massaged her right temple where a headache was beginning to slowly throb.

Molly stirred sugar into her tea and nudged the sugar bowl toward Sarah. "What happened?"

"Nothing out of the ordinary." Sarah spooned sugar into her own tea and gave Molly a weary half smile. "She didn't want to see the speech therapist, she refused to eat her lunch, she demanded that she be allowed to have her bridge club visit with her at their regular club time instead of visiting hours, and she refused to have anyone but me feed her dinner."

Molly rolled her eyes in disgust. "That sounds like Patricia. She's always been a pain in the—uh, always been difficult. I don't know why I thought she might behave herself when she's ill." She took a fat cookie from the plate and handed it to Sarah. "Here, you look like you need the calories."

"Thanks." The two sipped their tea and ate cookies in companionable silence for a few moments. "Did J.J. behave himself today?"

"Oh, sure," Molly said. "That boy belongs on a farm. Wes took J.J. and Caitlin with him on the tractor for an hour or two, then they went in the pickup to check on the pumps in a couple of pastures. I think they must have waded in mud around the water tanks because they came back dirty and wet, but happy as can be."

Sarah smiled and sipped her tea. "It sounds like J.J.'s idea of heaven. Did he go to bed without arguing?"

"Going to bed wasn't a problem—he was worn out. He still balked at taking a bath, but Caitlin told him she wouldn't read him a story if he wasn't clean, so he gave in without too much trouble."

Sarah laughed softly. "Talk about being caught between a rock and a hard place. J.J. is going through a stage where he hates taking baths, but he absolutely loves having Caitlin read to him."

"I know." Molly grinned, her lined face lighting with mischief. "I told you Caitlin was good with him." Her grin faded and was replaced by a small frown. "Her black eye is nearly gone. Did she ever tell you how she got it?"

Sarah shook her head. "No, but I think Margaret's boyfriend must have had something to do with it."

"Hmmph," Molly snorted in disgust. "What a prize he must be! And why would Margaret let him do something like that?"

"I don't know," Sarah answered. "But Caitlin told me she won't go back to L.A. until he's out of her mother's house. And I don't want Caitlin to go back at all."

"You're thinking of keeping her?"

"Yes," Sarah said firmly. "I am."

"Good." Molly nodded sharply. "That's the best news I've heard all week. In fact, Wes and I were just talking about that very thing yesterday. We'd ask Margaret to let Caitlin live with us, but we're pretty old to be parents to a teenager."

"You're not old, Molly," Sarah denied.

"Wes and I are more than old enough to be that

child's grandparents.'' Molly grinned and tugged at a silvery curl. ''And I earned every one of these gray hairs. Caitlin would be better off living with a younger person—like you, Sarah. But you're a single parent already. Are you sure you want to take on the responsibility of rearing another child alone?''

''I'm not sure how good a parent I would be for Caitlin, but having her in my home couldn't be worse for her than the situation with Margaret.''

''True. I swear, Margaret needs to look for a better class of men friends if the ones she's dating are into hitting little girls!''

''That's exactly what Josh said,'' Sarah said absently as she popped the last of her cookie into her mouth. Too late she realized what she'd said, and glanced quickly at her aunt. Molly was staring at her in wide-eyed surprise.

Chapter Four

"Josh? Josh Hightower?" Molly's voice reflected
her surprise. "When did you talk to Josh?"

Sarah hadn't meant to mention Josh to Molly.
Her aunt knew that she'd loved Josh five years before, but she'd never told the older woman what
had happened in Great Falls to cause the end of
their relationship. She chewed the cookie slowly
before swallowing, stalling for time while she considered just how much she wanted to tell Molly.

"Tonight, at the hospital," she finally answered.
"Murphy Redman is in a room down the hall from
mother's. He was kicked by a horse and broke his
leg."

"Oh, that poor man!" Molly was instantly sympathetic. "How bad was it?"

"Josh said the doctor told him that Murphy would be riding again in six months."

"Thank goodness," Molly said with relief before her gaze sharpened over Sarah's features. "So Josh was friendly?"

"Of course," Sarah answered innocently. "Why wouldn't he be?"

"Don't give me that innocent look," Molly said bluntly. "Those Hightower boys aren't known for forgiving and forgetting. I wouldn't have guessed that Josh Hightower would be inclined to speak to you at all, unless it was to yell at you. Five years ago that man nearly took this county apart when you left him and moved to Great Falls."

Sarah's fingers closed punishingly around her teacup. "I didn't know," she whispered painfully. For months, the only person from Butte Creek that she had had contact with was her mother, and Patricia had refused to discuss Josh.

"Didn't your mother tell you about the time she called the sheriff when Josh knocked on her door and demanded that she tell him where to find you?"

"No." Sarah shook her head. "No, she didn't. She never mentioned him at all. When I asked, she refused to talk about him."

"Hmmph." Molly's blue eyes snapped with disapproval. "That sounds like Patricia. She always has been a snob, and she never approved of your dating one of Will Hightower's boys."

Silence stretched while Sarah stared unseeingly at the tabletop.

"I was surprised when you moved away so suddenly, Sarah." Molly's voice was gentle. "I'll never forget how happy you seemed the few times I saw you with Josh. In fact, I told Wes what a pleasure it was to see a young couple so obviously in love. Was I wrong?"

"No." Sarah shook her head slowly. "No, you weren't wrong."

"What happened? Did you quarrel, did he do something to hurt you—"

"No." Sarah's swift denial was accompanied by a firm shake of her head. "Josh didn't do anything wrong, Molly. It was me...something happened and I couldn't..." She paused and drew a deep, tearing breath. "It wasn't Josh's fault."

"Then you aren't angry with him?"

"No. He did nothing to deserve what happened."

Molly's kind face was perplexed. "He hasn't dated anyone, as far as I know, since you left, Sarah. Perhaps the two of you might..."

Sarah shook her head adamantly. "No, there's no chance of our getting back together, Molly."

"But, why—"

"There just isn't, Molly. Some things aren't fixable. We're better off as we are."

The look Molly gave her was unconvinced, but to Sarah's relief, her aunt sighed and abandoned the subject. It wasn't long before the older woman gave her a warm hug and left for home and her husband.

Sarah waved good-night and wearily headed upstairs for her bed.

Some things aren't fixable. Exhausted though her body was, her mind was awake, replaying the conversation with her aunt. How she wished that her aunt was right, but she alone knew how impossible it was to hope for a relationship with Josh.

"Mommy, can we go see the horses?" J.J. bounced eagerly in the passenger seat, twisting to look out the window toward the barn.

"Yes, but don't go inside the corral," Sarah cautioned.

The car had barely stopped moving before J.J. was tugging at his seat belt and pushing open the door. Caitlin was faster and already out of the back seat, waiting impatiently by the car, when J.J. jumped out beside her.

"Dinner will be ready soon," Sarah called after them across the roof of the car. "Don't go farther than the barn."

"We won't," they chorused as they raced off.

Sarah smiled with wry affection and reached back into the car for a bag of groceries. She shifted it onto her hip, slammed the car door and headed for the kitchen. Caitlin and J.J. were fascinated by the horses and the activity of the men at the barn and corrals. Each morning Sarah dropped the two

at Molly's house on her way to the hospital, and
each afternoon when they returned to the Rocking
D, the little boy and girl raced off to the barn. There
they scrambled up the corral poles to perch on the
top rail and watch the men and horses with wide-
eyed fascination.

Molly's right, she reflected as she climbed the
porch steps. *Both J.J. and Caitlin are having the
time of their lives trailing after Uncle Wes at his
ranch and watching Josh with the horses here.*

Remaining in Butte Creek hadn't been even a
remote consideration when she left Great Falls, but
she was forced to think about the possibility in light
of Josh's astounding interest in fatherhood. If blood
tests proved that J.J. was his, she doubted that Josh
would be satisfied to have his son living perma-
nently across the width of the state. Nor could she
see herself denying either J.J. or Josh the opportu-
nity to spend as much time together as possible.
How she was going to come to terms with her own
feelings for Josh and deal with seeing him daily for
J.J.'s sake was a question for which she had no
answer.

Sarah sighed and dropped her purse, keys and the
bag of groceries on the kitchen table. She took time
to fill the kettle at the tap, set it on the stove and
measure loose tea into the teapot before removing
vegetables and salad greens from the bag. Alone in
the kitchen, she browned pork chops, chopped salad
ingredients and put broccoli on to steam. The fa-

miliar chores calmed her, distracting her troubled thoughts.

If Sarah had taken the time to look out her kitchen window at the corrals, she wouldn't have been concentrating on dinner.

Inside the foreman's house Rum surged to his feet expectantly when Josh finally hung up the phone and sighed with relief. The client on the other end of the line was ready, willing and able to pay top dollar for one of Baby's colts, but the garrulous man had a tendency to keep Josh on the telephone far longer than necessary to conduct business.

Josh stood and stretched before bending to stroke the big dog's head. "It's a good thing you can't talk, Rum, because I've had all the conversation I can stand for one day."

Rum's ears lifted at Josh's words; his head cocked sideways, eyes bright with intelligence. The black Lab loped happily at Josh's side when he shoved open the screen door and strode across the porch to return to the corrals, where he'd left Baby some forty minutes before.

J.J.'s excited shriek reached Josh's ears before he descended the last porch step. He frowned, lengthening his stride.

What the hell are those kids up to?

He strode past the edge of the grove that blocked sight of the corral and broke into a run, swearing aloud. J.J. was perched atop the corral rails, but Caitlin was inside the fence with Baby. Worse yet, she was riding the big horse bareback, and each jolting step he took sent her slipping to one side.

Josh didn't waste time opening the gate; he climbed the rails and vaulted over the top, dropping into the soft, powdery corral dust with a jolt he felt all the way up to his clenched jaw.

"Whoa, Baby," he crooned, his soft voice belying the anger that tightened his jaw and narrowed his eyes. "Easy, boy, slow down."

The big horse slowed from the rough trot to a walk, coming to an abrupt halt that jolted Caitlin forward, a good six inches of daylight visible between her jeans-clad bottom and his glossy back before she dropped with a thud. Josh caught Baby's mane with one hand.

"Get off him," he growled.

Caitlin unwound her fingers from Baby's rough mane and sat back, warily eyeing Josh.

"I didn't hurt him," she began. "I just…"

Josh didn't have enough patience to listen to her denial. He reached up, wrapped one hand around her arm and in one swift motion pulled her off the horse's back.

"Hey," she said belligerently. "Let go of me! You son of a— You can't…"

Baby shifted nervously, his eyes rolling as her voice rose in anger. Outside the corral, Rum's deep-throated barks added to the noise, and the quarter horse sidestepped and tossed his head, nearly jerking away from Josh's grip.

Josh released Baby's mane and headed for the gate, dragging Caitlin with him.

"Damn you! Let go of me this minute!" Caitlin pried at his fingers with no success. His implacable grip on her arm was like iron and he ignored her protests and flailing arms, dragging her from the corral despite her refusal to cooperate. It wasn't until the gate was closed and latched behind them that he released her and fixed her with an angry glare.

"What the hell were you doing on the back of that horse?" Josh demanded, his voice harsh with anger.

"I was riding him." Caitlin fisted her hands at her sides and glared back at him. "So what?"

"He's not your horse. Who gave you permission to ride him?"

"Nobody. I wanted to, so I did."

Josh leaned over her until they were nearly nose-to-nose. "You ever go near that horse again," he began with restrained fury, "and you'll be one sorry little girl."

Caitlin's face went pale beneath her tan. "Oh, yeah?" she said, her voice belligerent. "What are you going to do—hit me? Big deal. I've been hit before."

Her words shocked Josh and with sudden clarity he saw the genuine fear that lay beneath the cocky facade. "I didn't say I'd hit you," he said with irritation, his anger defused. "But I'm likely to paddle your butt till you can't sit down for a week."

Her response was a string of swearwords that were so creative that Josh could only stare at her, speechless.

"You can't hit her!" J.J. yelled. He let go of the post and scrambled down the corral rails to hurl himself at Josh. "Leave her alone!"

Inside the ranch house, Sarah stopped peeling vegetables at J.J.'s yell, and dropped the knife and potato into the sink to run for the front door. She reached the edge of her porch just in time to see Josh peel J.J. away from his leg and hold the squirming, shouting little boy at arm's length. Caitlin stood to one side, waving her arms and yelling obscenities at the top of her lungs. Beside her, Josh's big black Lab stood with tail erect, his deep, booming barks adding an underlying bass to the uproar.

Oh, no, Sarah groaned inwardly, running toward the corral. *What have those two done now?* "J.J.! Stop that this minute!"

Distracted by her voice, Josh shifted his attention from J.J.'s fierce attack to Sarah. Her hair was disheveled, her cheeks flushed from running, her eyes bright with worry as she ran toward them.

J.J. chose that moment to take advantage of Josh's lack of attention to land a glancing kick against his captor's shin.

"Knock that off," Josh said sternly, tightening his grip and shifting J.J. a little farther away.

"You can't hit Caitlin! You leave her alone!"

J.J.'s defense of his cousin was fearless. Josh stared at the little boy; there was something about the expression on his face and the set of J.J.'s jaw that strongly reminded Josh of his brother, Lucas. Despite the stinging pain in his shin, he was grudgingly forced to admit that he admired J.J.'s headlong launch into battle to defend Caitlin.

Breathless, Sarah reached the noisy group and grabbed J.J.'s arm, tugging him away from Josh. Caitlin abruptly snapped her mouth closed, cutting off a string of curse words in midsentence. The twelve-year-old eyed her aunt, her green eyes going from militant fury to dismay as she read her aunt's expression.

Sarah's hand closed more firmly over J.J.'s shoulder. "Stop squirming, J.J." Her glance flicked over Caitlin's guilty expression and J.J.'s obstinate little face before moving to Josh. "What did they do?"

J.J. burst into indignant speech before Josh could reply. "He was going to hit Caitlin!"

"Hush, J.J.," Sarah said firmly.

"I wasn't going to hit her," Josh growled with irritation. "I told her I'd paddle her rear if I ever caught her riding Baby again."

Sarah's eyes rounded in shock; one glimpse of Caitlin's guilty but still defiant expression confirmed his words. "Oh, no," she groaned. "Caitlin, you didn't! Whatever possessed you?"

"I only rode him around the corral," she said defensively. "I wouldn't have taken him outside the gate."

"That's not the point. Baby is a very valuable horse—not to mention the fact that stud horses are notoriously unpredictable. You could have been hurt. You don't even know the basics of horseback riding."

"But I'll never learn if I don't get on a horse," she protested. "And besides, Baby is a pussycat. He wouldn't hurt me."

"He could have hurt you without meaning to," Josh interjected. "You were slipping sideways on his back. Another few steps and he would have shaken you loose. You could have been stepped on—or worse."

"I thought you said he was as gentle as a baby. Isn't that why you call him Baby?" Caitlin asked with suspicion.

"No, he's called Baby because Lucas gave him that nickname when he was born and it stuck. We've called him that ever since. He has a long registered name, but Baby is all we ever use."

"Oh." Caitlin looked past Josh's shoulder at the corral where the big horse stood watching them. Ears pricked forward with interest, he seemed docile and friendly. "He doesn't look mean."

"He isn't mean," Josh denied patiently. "But

he's a stud and, given the right circumstances, he can be unpredictable.''

Caitlin shoved her hands into her pockets, the soft curve of her mouth creating a disheartened, downward arc. ''But he let me pet him, and he didn't buck me off when I got on his back.'' She glanced up at Josh through the thick tangle of her black lashes. ''It was kinda scary when he started trotting, 'cause I thought I might bounce off, but before that, it was really fun.''

''Riding is fun, but you can't just climb on a horse like Baby and ride him. You have to learn how to ride first, preferably on an older, gentler horse.''

J.J.'s expression brightened at Josh's words. ''You can teach us! Then when we learn how, we can ride Baby!''

''No, you can't ride Baby,'' Josh said impatiently, frowning at J.J. ''He's not a saddle horse.''

''But you have other horses,'' Caitlin interjected. ''Isn't one of them a saddle horse that's old and gentle enough for us to ride?''

Josh narrowed his eyes over her hopeful face. Beside her, J.J.'s small features held the same expectant, barely restrained eagerness.

''What if I did have such a horse,'' he said slowly. ''And what if I agreed to teach you. What will you swap me for lessons?''

Caitlin looked down at J.J.; J.J. looked up at Caitlin. Twin little frowns of worry drew down their brows and they looked back at Josh.

"We could work for you," Caitlin offered.

"Yeah." Beside her, J.J.'s head nodded with vigorous agreement. "We could do stuff."

"What kind of stuff?" Josh asked.

"We could do chores—like Trey does," Caitlin said promptly.

"You're willing to shovel manure?"

Caitlin's instant grimace of distaste brought a smile, quickly hidden, to Sarah's lips.

"I guess so." She shot him a challenging glance from beneath her lashes. "Are you willing to give us lessons?"

Josh hid a smile of his own. Caitlin was prickly and defensive, but even at twelve, she displayed unconsciously feminine gestures that left no doubt that she was going to be a heartbreaker someday.

"I might be," he conceded. "How about you, J.J.? Are you willing to shovel manure or do some other chore that needs to be done around here in return for riding lessons?"

"Yup." The little boy nodded solemnly and drew an *X* across his chest with a stubby forefinger. "I promise."

"All right." Josh nodded his head abruptly. "But in addition to doing chores, there are two rules that you have to obey. Without question." He fixed the two with a stern gaze. "Neither of you go near Baby or the broodmares."

"We won't," the two chorused fervently, interrupting him. "We promise!"

"And secondly," he continued, switching his stare to Caitlin, "you have to stop swearing."

"Why?" Caitlin's hackles rose instantly. "I don't talk any different than any of the rest of my friends in L.A."

"I don't care how your friends talk in L.A.," Josh said bluntly. "You're in Montana now, and young ladies in Butte Creek don't use a curse word every two seconds. At least, not when I'm around. You know words that no twelve-year-old girl should ever have heard—let alone repeated."

Caitlin's features held stubborn rebellion; Josh thought she was going to refuse, but then she flicked a quick glance at Sarah and her face fell. Her green eyes were filled with reluctant contrition and an underlying, barely concealed misery when her gaze returned to Josh.

"I'll try, really I will," she agreed. "I already promised Aunt Sarah that I'd try not to swear so much, but it's a lot harder than I thought it would be."

"Hmm," Josh folded his arms across his chest. "Maybe while you're breaking the habit, we can compromise." He pulled a half-dozen metal washers from his pocket. "Hold out your hand." She complied and he dropped the washers into her palm. "There's an empty mason jar sitting on a shelf just inside the barn. Each time I hear you swear, you have to put a washer in the jar. For each washer in the jar, you owe me an extra chore—my choice.''

Caitlin eyed the washers, her gaze flicking from the shiny metal circles to Josh and back again before she nodded. "All right. It's a deal."

She held out her hand and he took it, her small hand disappearing inside his callused palm.

"I want some, too." J.J. held out his two hands, palms cupped.

Josh shoved his hat back on his head and eyed the determined little boy. "Are you swearing, J.J.?"

"Yup."

"J.J.!"

His mother's dismayed tone brought a guilty expression to his face. His small shoulders lifted in a shrug of apology. "Just sometimes, Mommy," he said, sending her an angelic grin before he looked back up at Josh. "But I might need some washers to put in the jar just in case I say a bad word."

"All right." Josh fought back a grin and shoved a hand in his jeans pocket for three washers. "There you go."

Sarah watched J.J.'s hand close into a fist over the shiny metal. She had mixed feelings about the bargain Josh had struck with the children. She was torn between wanting to keep J.J. away from Josh, and guilt that if J.J. *was* Josh's son, she had already deprived Josh of his company for four long years.

She also felt responsible for Caitlin and J.J. misbehaving. *Josh is being more than understanding,* she realized with sudden insight. His handling of the two demonstrated a knowledge of children and a care for their safety and feelings that was almost fatherly.

She instantly rejected the idea. She didn't want to accept and believe that she'd been wrong about Josh. That he not only might have wanted to claim J.J. at birth, but that he had an instinctive, natural way with children.

He looked up from J.J.'s enthusiastic counting of the metal washers and caught her glance.

The banked anger that flared in those blue depths took her breath. *He's still furious at me,* she realized, her heart sinking. He looked away from her and back at J.J., leaving Sarah's heart beating double time, her breathing ragged.

"I can give them lessons," she offered.

Three pairs of eyes suddenly focused on her.

"No! I want Josh to teach me!" J.J. instantly argued, swiftly aligning himself with his new hero.

Caitlin, too, took a step closer to Josh.

"Josh is a very busy man, J.J.," Sarah began, sighing inwardly at the stubborn set of her son's jaw.

"I'll make time," Josh interjected. The swift surge of emotion he'd felt when J.J. had stepped beside him and hooked an arm around his leg stunned him. He glanced down at the little boy; all he could see was the crown of his head, but the tight grip J.J. had on his knee left no doubt that the kid wasn't giving in. J.J.'s sturdy little body was plastered along the length of his leg and Josh knew a fierce pride that the boy had chosen to stand with him.

Sarah's gaze rose from J.J. to Josh; the implacable set of their jaws was uncannily similar, and for a moment she stared, jolted by the resemblance. Even then, she would have argued further, but the brief flash of dark emotion in Josh's eyes silenced her protest.

"All right," she said quietly. "But now, I think we've taken up enough of your time this afternoon." She held out her hand and J.J. reluctantly stepped toward her.

"Do you want us to shovel manure this afternoon?" Caitlin asked.

Josh dragged his gaze away from Sarah and looked down at the girl. "No, tomorrow will be soon enough."

"All right. We'll be here as soon as Aunt Sarah gets home from the hospital," she promised with businesslike briskness.

"Until then, you two come back to the house and let Josh get on with his work." Sarah tugged on J.J.'s hand. "Bye." She gave Josh a small, perfunctory smile. J.J. dragged his feet at first and trailed a step behind her, gazing back over his shoulder at Josh as they walked away. Caitlin trotted after them until she caught up with Sarah, then she slowed to keep pace with her aunt.

Josh stood, watching the three as they crossed the barn lot and disappeared into the house. A queer ache lodged just beneath his breastbone; J.J. skipped and hopped, holding his mother's hand, chattering nonstop, while Sarah, her hair gleaming silver-blond beneath the hot afternoon sun, alternately bent to listen to J.J. or turned to speak to Caitlin. They created a charmed circle, and he felt left out, unbearably lonely at being excluded from their warmth.

Rum whined and shoved his wet nose into Josh's palm, demanding his attention.

"What's the matter, boy?" Josh smoothed his hand over the big dog's fur. Rum whined again, tail wagging as he gazed at the ranch house's empty doorway. "They'll be back to play with you tomorrow. Till then you'll just have to make do with me."

The Lab gazed sadly up at him; his tail and even his ears seemed to droop.

"You're pitiful, Rum." Josh turned purposefully toward the corral, the big dog walking disconsolately beside him. "I hate to admit it, but you remind me of myself."

Josh ignored the emotions roiling in him, as usual, from any contact with Sarah, and returned to work.

* * *

Sarah couldn't sleep. The memory of Josh smiling down at J.J. tortured her and she tossed and turned, tangling and twisting the sheets until she finally threw them aside in irritation and slipped out of bed. Moonlight threw a bar of pale light across the floor, and Sarah padded through its cool glow to stand at the window. Outside, the night was as quiet as the house, still and silent under the light from the half-moon.

Too restless to bear the confinement of four walls, Sarah pulled the light blanket from her bed and left the room. The big grandfather clock in the hall struck midnight just as she tugged open the door and stepped out onto the porch.

The night air was chill; goose bumps rose on her arms and legs, left bare by the thigh-length, scoopnecked, sleeveless cotton nightie she wore. Sarah swung the soft blue blanket around her shoulders for warmth as she padded barefoot across the cool porch boards. The white wooden swing creaked when she sat, the chains uttering a soft groan of metal link against metal link as they took her weight. She swung her feet up onto the seat and tucked the blanket around them, nestling inside the warm cocoon of blue cotton.

What am I going to do about Josh? The memory of his gentle smile as he gazed down at J.J. was just as vivid in the open air of the porch as it had been in her room. Still, it wasn't only his obvious affection for J.J. that was destroying her sleep. For the first time in five long years, Sarah struggled with physical attraction.

She squeezed her eyes shut and groaned silently. Ever since that fateful night when violence had altered her life forever, her primary reaction to men had been an overwhelming need to put as much distance as possible between herself and them. She'd become so accustomed to being frozen, both sexually and emotionally, that this thawing was shocking and painful. The violent reawakening of long-dormant sexual feelings was torture. Her body ached for Josh, and vivid memories of the times they'd made love refused to leave her alone, no matter how she tried to avoid them.

The memories of the passion they'd shared were torment, especially since she knew that even if he didn't hate her, she was incapable of physical contact—even with Josh.

The muffled clip-clop of a horse's hooves reached her ears; Sarah's eyes opened and she searched the dark corral, but couldn't see the black bulk of a horse.

The sound grew louder and she realized that it was coming from the lane that led to the county road.

What in the world? Frowning, she leaned forward to scan the lane. A lone rider moved slowly toward the ranch buildings, the dark shadow of a big dog trotting beside the bigger bulk of the horse. The trio was yards away from the house when the smaller form of the dog left the horse's side and loped toward the porch. Within seconds Rum nudged his nose against Sarah's blanket-covered feet and softly whined a greeting, his tail wagging with delight.

"Rum?" She smoothed her palm over his big head, and he responded by wagging his tail even harder. Her gaze raced to the rider sitting motionless atop the black horse, and for one wildly fanciful moment she thought her tortured desire had summoned him from the night.

Josh halted Baby outside the open gate. Rum was standing beside the porch swing, his black coat making him nearly invisible in the shadows; a blanket-wrapped figure was curled up on the wide seat.

"Josh?"

Sarah's voice was hushed, carrying undertones of disbelief and bewilderment.

Josh didn't answer. Unable to sleep, he'd finally saddled Baby and gone riding, but the hours he'd spent under the night sky had only tired his body; the physical exercise hadn't done a thing to lessen the restless, never-ending, hot need that drove him.

He dismounted, the saddle leather creaking as it shifted under his weight, and strode silently up the walk to the porch.

Sarah stared at him. He wasn't wearing a hat, and his black hair was mussed by the wind. Moonlight illuminated one side of his face, catching the gleam of his eyes beneath dark brows and the taut, hard line of his mouth. He took the steps two at a time and stalked to within a foot of the swing, a dangerous edginess charging the air around him. Sarah had to tilt her head back to look up at him, and she caught the scent of wind and sage mixed with the faint odor of leather, horse and aftershave.

"What are you doing out here—alone—in the middle of the night?" he demanded, his voice harsh.

"I couldn't sleep. I was worried about Mother." She uttered the white lie for self-protection without a twinge of guilt. "Why are you out?"

He stared at her for a long, charged moment. "I couldn't sleep."

"Oh."

Sarah heard her heart beat in time with the swift tick of the big old clock in the hall inside while Josh held her gaze for what felt like an eternity. Then he cursed under his breath and spun away from her to prowl across the porch to the railing.

"Too bad you aren't awake for the same reason I am," he said without turning.

"Oh? And what's that?"

He shifted to face her, leaning his hips against the railing and crossing his arms across his chest. With the moon at his back, his face was in shadows and Sarah couldn't read his expression.

"I was remembering how good you were in bed." He ignored Sarah's soft gasp. "And you were good, Sarah—better than good, you were incredible. I've never been with a woman who was quite so good at convincing the poor bastard she's with that she's out of her mind with pleasure. You should have gone on stage, Sarah. You're a great actress.''

"I wasn't acting."

"No?" His tone was bitterly self-derisive. "You mean all those little throaty moans I heard in my ear when I was buried inside you were real? You had me so crazy with wanting you that I would have taken you in the middle of Main Street in broad daylight.'' He slowly unfolded his arms and pushed away from the railing to move closer until he was looming over Sarah, his hands clenching the wood swing on each side of her, powerful arms bracketing her. "From the first time when I actually believed you were a virgin until the last time we were together, you had me completely convinced that I was the only man in your life," he snarled. "And we both know that's not true, don't we, Sarah?"

His face was only inches from hers. Wounded and dangerous, Josh radiated anger. His eyes gleamed with feral heat in a face that held no softness or gentle consideration, only hard angles and the unrelenting fury of betrayal.

Still, it didn't occur to Sarah to be afraid of him.

"I'm sorry, Josh." A wealth of emotion, regret and impending tears filled her voice. "I'm so sorry.''

Her eyes were dark pools of pain in the pale oval of her face close beneath his, the soft curve of her mouth trembling. Josh's fingers clenched over the wood boards of the swing as he fought the urge to drop his head and cover her lips with his.

"Telling me you're sorry is too little and way too late," he finally said, his voice rough with the effort it cost him to speak. "It was too late when you left my bed for someone else's."

He forced his fingers to release the wooden slats of the swing, his movements jerky as he pulled his arms away and straightened. He strode across the porch, one hand closing with punishing force over the support post next to the steps.

"Josh, I didn't..." Without conscious thought, Sarah was out of the seat and across the porch, her hand reaching for his bare forearm. She grabbed the porch post instead, unable to actually touch him.

He jerked, his big body going stiff, the muscles in his arm jumping in reaction. He turned slowly and looked at her. Wild, out-of-control emotion raged in his eyes and Sarah froze, suddenly aware that the near touch of her hand had pushed him over some invisible line—and that he was dangerous.

"But you did." The words were barely audible, spoken as they were through clenched teeth. "Damn you, Sarah."

Swift as a striking cobra, he caught the back of her head in one big hand, his fingers fisting in her hair to hold her still, and his mouth dropped to cover hers.

Sarah didn't have time to protest. He didn't touch her except for his hand in her hair and his lips against hers. For endless seconds his mouth punished hers, the pressure of his kiss forcing her head back against his palm. Suddenly his mouth gentled against hers, moving with slow, drugging persuasion while his lips relearned the taste, textures and sensitive curves of hers.

She was drowning in sensation, the world narrowed to the coaxing, arousing movements of his mouth against hers.

Just as abruptly as he'd taken her, Josh ripped his mouth away. She staggered, disoriented by the sudden shift from sensual fever to awareness, her fingers clenched over the porch post.

He stepped back. "That was a mistake." He ground the words out harshly, his breathing fast and heavy, loud in the still night air. "It won't happen again." He turned and strode swiftly away, mounting Baby and riding away without looking back.

Would it have hurt him less if I'd told him the truth? Sarah dropped onto the swing and watched him go, unaware that tears coursed down her cheeks. *Would he hate me less if he knew that I was raped?*

Sarah stared, unseeing, at the moonlit, silent cluster of buildings. She was remembering herself checking in to a motel in Great Falls five years ago.

She hadn't heard the man behind her, didn't know she had been followed from the check-in counter at the motel office until the man forced her inside her room. He ripped her purse and car keys out of her hand, but when he began tearing at her clothes she fought back. The ensuing assault was brutal, leaving her unconscious from a blow to the head.

When she was found by the motel cleaning staff two days later, she was still drifting in and out of consciousness from a concussion. She reacted hysterically to any male that came near her, from the EMTs to the hospital staff doctors. Contacted by the police, her mother rushed to her side.

When she was released from the hospital, Patricia rented a small house to enable Sarah to attend the intensive therapy designed to help her deal with the trauma of the attack. Emotionally distraught, consumed with shame and guilt, Sarah was unable to face Josh and had contact with no one except her mother, her counselors and her doctors. It wasn't until three weeks later that she realized she was pregnant; her mother immediately insisted that she have an abortion, but Sarah refused. She didn't know if Josh or her attacker had fathered the child, and she couldn't bring herself to destroy a baby that she and Josh might have created. Patricia finally conceded that Sarah's emotional and physical health was too shaky to face such a decision, but insisted that her daughter give the child up for adoption at birth.

Sarah had felt confident that she would know immediately if Josh were the father when her child was born. The genes that gave Josh his crow black hair and deep blue eyes would surely dominate over the genes that carried her own silvery blond hair and blue eyes. But by the time she'd carried the child in her womb for nine long months, she knew that regardless of the identity of the father, she couldn't bear to give her baby to another woman to love and raise. Unfortunately for her peace of mind, her little boy was born with distinctive, unfamiliar tiptilted green eyes and Sarah's silver-blond hair, and didn't look like either Josh or the man who had assaulted her.

Furious at Sarah's determination to keep the baby, Patricia told her that she would have to stay in Great Falls, because she couldn't bring the child home to Butte Creek. Patricia's reputation would be ruined, the disgrace unbearable.

Sarah acceded to her mother's ultimatum, but only because she knew that she couldn't live near Josh. She loved him deeply, but was still unable, even after intensive therapy, to endure physical contact with a male. It had taken months for her to control the instinct to flee from men, or flinch from the most innocent of contact. She was convinced that she would never be normal, never be able to satisfy Josh in an intimate, male-female relationship.

Beyond that, she couldn't bring herself to face

Josh and tell him that she'd been raped. The barely concealed disgust she'd seen on her mother's face when she'd awakened in the hospital had been devastating. She couldn't bear to see the same shock and accusation on the face of the man she loved.

She was also convinced that he wouldn't want her now that she had a child. Well aware of the damage done to Josh by his father's alcoholism and his mother's desertion of the family when he was barely four, Sarah had understood why he was so adamantly set against having a family of his own. Still, she'd been sure she could change his mind with enough time and love—but that possibility was destroyed by the assault and her pregnancy.

Josh hadn't wanted children, and Sarah could never give up her baby. Josh was an intensely passionate man, and Sarah could no longer bear to be touched.

Nearly a year had passed before she had finally given up all hope that she could find a solution that would allow her any hope for a future with Josh. She'd written to him—a carefully polite, purposely vague letter, in which she told him that she had moved on with her life, and that she hoped he had, too.

Four years had gone by before her mother suffered her stroke and Sarah had been forced to return to Butte Creek and face Josh.

She'd known it was going to be hard, but she'd badly misjudged just how difficult it would be.

Sarah sighed and brushed a hand across her face, surprised at the dampness on her fingers and palm. Inside the house, the clock chimed the hour and she pushed herself upright, staring out over the dark land.

If she told Josh the truth, would he be less tormented by a past they couldn't change or make right? Would he hate her any less for denying him knowledge of J.J. if tests proved that the little boy wasn't his biological son?

The dark night held no answers, and only stillness met her silent, anguished cry.

Sarah left the waning moon behind. It wasn't until she was in bed and nearly asleep that she realized she hadn't panicked when Josh kissed her. Stunned, she sat upright in bed and struggled to understand what had happened. Not only had he kissed her, but he'd wound his fingers in her hair and held her captive—and she hadn't fought wildly to be released. Nor had she been truly afraid of him. On some basic, subconscious level, she trusted him.

What did it mean? Was there a possibility that she was incapable of physical contact only with men other than Josh?

Tolerating a kiss is minor compared to actually making love. Sarah forced herself to face the likelihood that she'd been caught off guard by the swiftness of Josh's forced kiss—and the fact that it had been over nearly as soon as it had begun.

Practicality quenched the brief flash of hope and

she lay down again, pulled the covers up beneath her chin and ordered her racing mind to cease its struggles and let her exhausted body rest.

Over the next several days J.J. and Caitlin, happily shadowed by Rum, raced off to the barn to find Josh the moment Sarah brought them home each afternoon. Although Josh had a three-year-old nephew, he hadn't quite realized what he was letting himself in for when he'd told J.J. and Caitlin that they could do chores in exchange for riding lessons. He'd visualized a simple job or two a day; the kids, however, zealously pursued him for job assignments from the moment they got home until Sarah called them for dinner. He was hard-pressed to find enough to keep them busy without endangering them, particularly the determined J.J.

Sarah was well aware that her son could be a handful, and the relatively short time that she'd spent with Caitlin had taught her that the twelve-year-old could be difficult without half trying.

Her curiosity as to how Josh was coping with the junior dynamos had her strolling to the barn late one afternoon to call the children for dinner, instead of ringing the old dinner bell on the porch. Caitlin was perched on the top rail of the corral, Zach Colby's tall figure leaning against the rails beside her. Inside the corral, J.J. was in the saddle atop a brown gelding, his eyes bright with excitement while Josh led the horse in slow circles.

"Faster! Faster!" he demanded. Josh obediently walked a little faster, the gelding plodding a little more quickly behind him.

Sarah reached the corral and leaned her forearms along the top of a rail to watch. "How's he doing?"

Caitlin twisted to look down at her, a quick grin curving her mobile mouth upward and echoing the sparkle in her green eyes.

"Hi, Aunt Sarah." She glanced back at J.J. "He hasn't fallen off yet. Josh won't let him take the reins by himself until he stops bouncing around in the saddle."

"Ahh." Sarah nodded in understanding. Her gaze went past Caitlin to Zach Colby's profile. "Good afternoon, Zach."

The tall rancher turned his head to look at her, his ice blue eyes remote.

"Afternoon, Sarah." The brief acknowledging nod he gave her was polite but reserved.

Sarah nodded in return and turned back to watching J.J. She'd met Zach Colby several times when she and Josh had been dating, because he was Josh's best friend. Although Zach had always been an enigma, she didn't remember that he had ever been quite so abrupt. His attitude just now had bordered on rude.

Maybe Josh isn't the only one who hates me, she thought bleakly.

Josh was aware that Sarah was standing outside the corral fence. He seemed to have built-in radar that picked up her presence wherever she was on the ranch, but he was grimly determined to fight that awareness. The midnight encounter on her porch had taught him just how easily she could push him over the edge and destroy his self-control. He didn't plan to let it happen again.

"All right, J.J." He halted the horse. "That's all for today. Now it's Caitlin's turn."

"Aw, Josh," J.J. pleaded. "Can't we go around just one more time?"

"Nope." Josh dropped the reins, ground-hitching the gelding. The little boy sat solidly atop the adult saddle, his legs dangling two feet above the stirrups, his small hands gripping the saddle horn. Josh reached up and caught him around the waist; J.J. reluctantly let go of the saddle horn and let Josh swing him to the ground.

"Can I ride him again tomorrow?" he asked, head tilted back to look up.

"Sure." Josh knew he had at least twenty hours of work that he needed to get done in only ten hours the next day, but he found himself agreeing anyway. The hopeful intensity of the green eyes in the small, earnest face tugged at his heart, and the swift delight that lit J.J.'s face was reward enough. For what seemed the thousandth time, he searched for similarities between himself and J.J., wondering if they shared the same blood—wondering how good a father he'd be if they did.

Sarah barely noticed Caitlin as she climbed down

from the corral fence and ran toward Josh. She was too intent on the man and little boy across the width of the powdery arena floor. Whatever J.J. had asked Josh, his response had the little boy grinning with delight. What stopped her heart, however, was the slow, gentle pass of Josh's palm over J.J.'s ruffled cap of silver-blond hair, his fingers smoothing the tousled strands. There was something so inherently, yearningly parental in the gesture that a lump of emotion choked her throat. How many times had she made that very gesture? J.J. thought himself too old for the many hugs she wanted to give him, but untold times during the day he allowed her that simple caress without protest.

"Mommy!" J.J. pelted across the corral and scrambled between the bottom two rails. "I get to ride Tornado tomorrow! Did you see me? Did you see me?"

He tugged on her skirt, demanding her attention.

"Yes, I saw you. I saw you," she repeated when he bounced up and down, repeating his question.

"I'm going to ride just like Josh someday," J.J. said firmly. "And Tornado is going to run just like Baby."

Sarah flicked a startled glance at Zach. "Tornado?" She glanced back at the horse in the corral. The gelding stood quietly, his eyes half-closed, wisps of hay protruding from each side of his mouth while he chewed methodically. She looked back at Zach, and his blue eyes held a touch of humor that melted some of the ice.

"Tornado," he drawled in confirmation. "His original owner named him that. I think the man had a sense of humor."

Across the arena, Josh stood motionless, watching Sarah smile at Zach, while a fierce twist of jealousy stabbed through his gut.

"You might as well forget it."

Caitlin's hostile tone brought his head swinging around. The twelve-year-old sat atop the horse, staring down at him with an aggressive expression, her deep green eyes narrowed with displeasure.

"What are you talking about?" he asked, his own eyes narrowed over her.

"Aunt Sarah," the girl said bluntly. "Leave her alone."

Chapter Five

Josh stared at Caitlin, frowning fiercely. "Just what do you mean by that?"

"I saw the way you were looking at her," she said curtly. "I've seen my mother's boyfriends look at her just the same way, but my mom is tough, she can handle men. Aunt Sarah's nice—and she doesn't need you causing trouble for her."

Josh's frown turned into a glare. "For a twelve-year-old, you've got some pretty adult ideas."

Shaded with weary cynicism, her green eyes met his without flinching. "I may be only twelve, but that doesn't mean I'm an idiot. You leave Aunt Sarah alone," she repeated determinedly.

Josh continued to meet her stare with his own.

He hadn't told her she was wrong, because he suspected that she had easily read on his face the hunger that clawed at him every time he looked at Sarah. Given Caitlin's background with Margaret, he wasn't surprised by her shrewdly mature assessment.

"I don't plan to do anything that would hurt Sarah," he said finally.

She stared down at him for a brief, telling moment before her gaze flicked from him to her aunt. "All right." She straightened, poker stiff, in the saddle. "Do I still get my lesson?" She didn't look at him when she asked, focusing intently on the gelding's ears.

"We made a deal," Josh said shortly. "You're not supposed to swear, but I don't remember your agreeing not to be an interfering pain in the butt."

Caitlin sucked in a breath, her eyes wide with surprise when her gaze flew to his face.

"Pay attention," he growled, and began to explain the proper method of neck-reining.

For once in her life, Caitlin was silenced, concentrating intently as he demonstrated.

The three watching the lesson couldn't hear the conversation, but Sarah could almost see the waves of hostility coming off first Caitlin, and then Josh. She didn't realize she was holding her breath until Josh began to demonstrate reining to Caitlin. Her breath eased out in a heavy sigh; clearly, whatever they'd been bristling about had been resolved.

* * *

Whatever Josh had said to Caitlin during her first riding lesson, she wasn't telling. Sarah tried to get the girl to discuss it, but gave up when Caitlin stonewalled and grew stubbornly silent.

Patricia was growing stronger each day. It was only two days after the lesson that Sarah decided her mother was well enough to allow a visit with J.J. and Caitlin.

"Mommy, why is Grandma Patricia in the hospital?" J.J. queried as they walked down the hall toward her room.

"Because she had a stroke," Sarah explained for the tenth time that afternoon. "And she has to stay here until she's well again."

Beside J.J., Caitlin fidgeted nervously, her fingers twisting the loose end of her braid. Sarah caught the small fingers in her own and smiled encouragingly into Caitlin's apprehensive green eyes.

"She won't like me," Caitlin said, the words coming out in a rush as they stopped in front of the door to Patricia's room.

"Of course she will," Sarah said reassuringly. "What makes you think she won't?"

Caitlin shrugged and tugged at her ear, fingering the simple studs—only two per ear—that gleamed silver against the soft skin of her lobe. "Margaret told me she wouldn't. Not that I care," she added hastily with an unconvincing shrug. "But I might forget and swear if she yells at me, and I already have four metal washers in Josh's jar.''

Sarah saw past the bravado to the vulnerable little girl inside. ''Your grandmother isn't going to yell at you, Caitlin. She's been very ill and has difficulty speaking. Even when she's well, your grandmother Patricia can be...difficult, but if you're patient and let her get to know you, she can't help but love you.''

''Do you think so?''

''I know so,'' Sarah said, silently praying that Patricia was having one of her good days and wouldn't say anything sharply cutting to her granddaughter.

''All right.'' Caitlin drew a deep breath, her gaze shifting to the closed door.

''Good girl.'' Sarah glanced around to find J.J. investigating the rubber wheels on a cart a few feet away. ''Come here, J.J.''

The little boy reluctantly left his perusal of the metal brake on the wheel and skipped back to his mother. Sarah knocked briefly before pushing open the door.

''Hello, Mother.''

Patricia lay in the elevated hospital bed, reclining against several pillows. Her silvery-gold hair was brushed neatly, her makeup smoothly applied. Were it not for the faint downward twist to the left side of her face and mouth and the wires that attached her to the heart monitor, she might have been ready to receive visitors in her own home.

Her pale blue eyes narrowed over J.J. and Caitlin before her gaze flicked to Sarah.

"I've brought your grandchildren to visit, Mother," Sarah said. Refusing to react to the lack of response in her mother's silent stare, she took both children by the hand and approached the bed. "Don't you think J.J.'s grown since you visited us in the spring? And this is Caitlin." She drew her niece forward to stand in front of her, cupping her hands over Caitlin's thin shoulders and shifting closer so that they touched lightly, her front to Caitlin's back, in a subtly protective gesture. "Caitlin, this is your grandmother Patricia. She hasn't seen you since you were two years old and your mother moved to Los Angeles."

"Good afternoon, Grandmother." Caitlin's voice was carefully polite, her hands folded meekly in front of her.

Sarah held her breath while her mother's sharp gaze traveled assessingly over Caitlin's face and slender body. At last Patricia lifted a slim white hand and beckoned her nearer.

Caitlin stiffened under Sarah's clasp before she stepped forward, halting when her thighs lightly brushed against the soft blue blanket.

Patricia caught Caitlin's chin in a surprisingly strong grip and tilted her face toward the window and the strong sunlight. For a long moment she stared at her granddaughter before she nodded abruptly and dropped her hand.

"You've got Margaret's cheekbones," she said slowly, carefully forming the words. "But those green eyes and that black hair never came from a Drummond."

"No, ma'am," Caitlin replied. "Margaret says I got them from my father."

"Let's hope that's all of your father he bred into you." Patricia's words were faintly slurred, but nonetheless sharp. "And why do you call your mother by her given name?"

"She asked me to," Caitlin answered, her voice edgy with growing resentment.

Patricia sniffed her displeasure. "I'm sure I don't know what's gotten into that daughter of mine," she said haltingly, struggling with the words. "It's completely inappro—inapprop—" She faltered, frustrated with her inability to form the longer word.

"Margaret is sometimes a little unconventional, Mother," Sarah interjected diplomatically; she could tell by Caitlin's narrowed green eyes and mutinous expression that her niece had exhausted her ability to be docile and polite in the face of her grandmother's criticism. She tugged J.J. forward. "Say hello to your grandmother, J.J."

"Hello, Grandma," J.J. responded dutifully.

Patricia's blue gaze softened, thawing almost imperceptibly as it rested on the little boy. "Good afternoon, J.J.,'' she said carefully. "How are your studies coming along?"

J.J.'s face brightened. "I can print my name," he answered, holding up both hands, fingers splayed. "And I can count to fifty."

Patricia smiled faintly, only the right side of her mouth moving upward. Her gaze switched to Caitlin. "Yours..."

"My studies?" Caitlin asked, waiting for Patricia's jerky nod of agreement before she answered. "I'm in an accelerated program. I skipped third and fifth grades and if I'd gone to summer school this year, I would have skipped another grade and entered eleventh grade this fall."

Patricia's gaze narrowed as if reassessing her granddaughter. Clearly, there was more to this child than the quadruple-pierced ears, the worn jeans, and the aggressively held chin had led her to believe.

Sarah realized that she was staring at Caitlin with her mouth open, and quickly snapped it shut. She'd known the child was intelligent, but Caitlin hadn't said anything before about being involved in what obviously was a Los Angeles program for gifted children.

Patricia lifted a hand to gesture at Caitlin's ears. "What—" she began, but a loud crash snapped her attention away from Caitlin.

Sarah spun away from the bed; J.J. stood near the small dresser, ice cubes dotting the pool of water spreading swiftly at his feet. A pink plastic water pitcher lay on its side on the waxed floor, but J.J. held the matching pink lid in one small fist.

"I'm sorry, Mommy," he said quickly, glancing guiltily at the spreading water. "I just wanted to get a drink."

Sarah groaned silently.

"I'll help him, Aunt Sarah," Caitlin offered. She hurried away from her grandmother. "Don't step in the water, J.J.," she warned as she disappeared into the bathroom.

"I won't." J.J. disappeared after her. "I can help."

"All right." Caitlin's voice carried clearly to the two women. "Here, you take these paper towels and I'll bring this."

The two emerged from the bathroom, J.J. rushing to drop his handful of paper towels in the midst of the puddle of water.

Caitlin went about disposing of the pool of water, and placed the heavy, hospital-issue brown paper towels into a small plastic pan.

Satisfied that Caitlin had the minor emergency well in hand, Sarah turned back to the bed and found Patricia intently watching the two children.

"She's very good with him," Sarah said, turning slightly to watch Caitlin supervise J.J.'s exuberant splashing of water from the wet towels into the pan.

Frowning, Patricia struggled to speak. "Ear... rings..."

Sarah knew exactly what her mother was trying

to say—the older woman hated Caitlin's double earrings. *Thank goodness she didn't notice that Caitlin has four holes per ear.* "I know, Mother, but Margaret let Caitlin have her ears pierced and must know that her daughter is wearing double earrings."

Patricia made a lopsided grimace of distaste. "Mar'gret never did...have any sense about fashion," she finally managed to get out.

"Aunt Sarah?" Caitlin waited until Sarah looked over her shoulder before continuing. "J.J. is thirsty. Can we look for a soda machine?"

J.J. jumped down from the chair he was exploring, his tennis shoes thumping loudly against the waxed linoleum floor. "Yeah, can we, Mommy?"

Sarah glanced at her mother, accurately read the growing frown and guessed that Patricia was about to lecture J.J. about noise and Caitlin about her earrings. "I think that's an excellent idea," she said hastily, reaching into the pocket of her shorts for change. "Here's some money, Caitlin. Why don't you try the cafeteria on the first floor. I'm sure you can find cold drinks there."

Caitlin's face lightened with subtle relief; she moved across the room to take the coins from Sarah. "Thank you, Aunt Sarah. I hope you're feeling better soon, Grandmother," she added politely.

Patricia managed an abrupt nod. Caitlin turned and caught J.J.'s small hand firmly in hers. J.J.

skipped along beside her as they hurried toward the hall.

"Caitlin," Sarah called as the two reached the doorway. Caitlin's ebony braid shifted forward over her shoulder as she looked inquiringly back at Sarah. "Would you bring me a cup of coffee when you come back?"

"Sure." A smile lit Caitlin's face and she and J.J. disappeared into the hall.

J.J. chattered happily, the sound of his voice drifting back into the room to reach Sarah's ears before fading away into silence.

For a moment Sarah wished wistfully that she could go with them, but then, sighing silently, she turned back to her mother and braced herself for the lecture she knew *she* was about to receive.

"Look! It's Josh!" J.J. exclaimed, his wide, gap-toothed grin white against his summer-tanned face as the two reached the room two doors down from their grandmother's. He tugged his hand free from Caitlin's grip and raced into the room. "Hi, Josh, what are you doing here?"

"Hi, J.J." The deep drawl of Josh's voice answered J.J.'s treble. "I'm visiting my friend Murphy. Murphy, meet J.J.—and Caitlin," he added as Caitlin stepped inside the room and halted. "What are you two doing at the hospital?"

"Mommy brought us to visit Grandma, but we're

thirsty so we're going to go downstairs to the caf'teria and get sodas.''

Caitlin took three steps forward and stopped, warily eyeing Josh.

Murphy was lying in a high hospital bed, his right leg elevated with pulleys and encased in a thick white cast. He looked at the children with interest.

"Wow! What did you do to your leg, mister?" J.J.'s eyes were round as he leaned against the side of the bed and stared with unabashed curiosity at the raised leg.

"Does it hurt?" Caitlin asked with a worried frown, forgetting about Josh as she walked closer to inspect the mechanical apparatus that kept the casted leg elevated.

"Nah," Murphy said with aplomb. "It looks a lot worse than it feels. I got kicked by a horse, but I'll be out of here and dancing in no time—maybe sooner, right, Josh?"

Arms crossed on his broad chest, Josh half sat on the window ledge, his booted feet crossed at the ankles, and watched the children with Murphy.

"Probably sooner," he drawled, answering Murphy's question. "But you won't be riding bucking horses at the county fair this summer."

"Hah." Murphy snorted in disgust. "I'm too old and too smart to ride rough stock, and you dam—" He stopped in midsentence and cast a swift, guilty glance at the children. "Dang well know it."

"Uh-oh, mister." J.J. shook his head at him. "You said a bad word. Now you'll have to put a washer in the jar and shovel horse poop."

Murphy stared at him, confused. "Huh? I have to do what?"

Josh chuckled, a rich, deep sound of amusement. "The kids and I have a contract, Murphy. I give them riding lessons on Tornado, and they don't ride Baby or the broodmares—and they don't swear."

"What in tarnation does that have to do with a washer in a jar and shoveling horse dung?" Perplexed, Murphy looked from J.J.'s solemn face to Caitlin's wide grin.

"If we swear, we have to put a washer in the jar in the barn, and then Josh gets to take the washer out and make us shovel horse poop to get it back," J.J. said seriously. "But you can't shovel stuff with your leg in that thing, so Josh will probably make you do something worse." Clearly concerned that Murphy was in big trouble, J.J.'s worried gaze went to Josh.

Josh fought to keep a straight face. "Maybe we should let Murphy off the hook this time, J.J. He didn't know the rules."

J.J. gave a judicious, relieved nod and turned back to Murphy. "It's okay, Mister Murphy." He leaned closer. "But don't forget, 'cause Josh really will make you shovel out the horse stalls."

"Okay." Murphy's face was grave, but his black eyes danced with amusement when they met Josh's.

"And you don't have to call me mister—just plain old Murphy will do. Speaking of shoveling out horse stalls, I'm reminded of the time I caught and broke wild mustangs. It was back in..."

Josh smiled, listening as Murphy started to spin one of his many stories. Fascinated, J.J. climbed up to perch on the edge of Murphy's bed and Caitlin settled on the arm of a nearby chair, both children finding seats without ever taking their eyes from Murphy.

Down the hall, Patricia had fallen asleep, her eyelids drifting closed to hide the frustration in her eyes. Sarah glanced at her watch, frowned, then rose quietly from her seat beside her mother's bed. More than a half hour had gone by, and J.J. and Caitlin hadn't returned.

She tiptoed across the room and stepped into the hall, pulling the door closed behind her. A burst of muted laughter reached her and she recognized J.J.'s delighted chuckle.

What in the world? She moved quickly down the hall and stopped abruptly at the second open door.

Murphy Redman was propped up in the bed, one leg heavily casted and elevated with a pulley mechanism. Perched on the edge of his bed was J.J., while Caitlin sat on the arm of a nearby chair. Both children were listening with wide-eyed fascination, enthralled by Murphy's animated storytelling.

Across the room, half leaning, half sitting on the

wide window ledge, was Josh. A lazy smile curved his lips as he watched Murphy wave his hands to underline his words.

Sarah stepped quietly into the room. Josh's gaze instantly flicked from Murphy toward the hall door and found her; his eyes widened in a brief, betraying movement and he stiffened before his expression went carefully blank.

Murphy glanced at Josh; the tense set of his body and austere lines of his face were clear indicators that something was wrong. Frowning, Murphy followed Josh's intent stare and discovered Sarah Drummond standing just inside the door.

"I'm sorry to interrupt." Sarah managed to ignore Josh's unwelcoming stare and walked toward the bed. "Are my children bothering you?"

"Your children?" Murphy shifted his puzzled gaze from Sarah's face to Caitlin and then to J.J. He glanced quickly from J.J.'s small face to Josh's set expression. "These are your children?"

"She's *my* Mommy," J.J. explained. "And she's Caitlin's aunt, but Caitlin's staying with us now and I want to keep her 'cause I don't have a sister and I need her to keep me company when we go back to Great Falls."

"I see," Murphy said thoughtfully. Once again his gaze lingered on J.J.'s features before moving assessingly to Josh's set face. He looked back at J.J. and smiled gently. "And what about your daddy? Did you leave him in Great Falls?"

"Nope," J.J. said with blithe unconcern. "We don't have a daddy."

Sarah tensed at Murphy's seemingly innocent question. She could feel Josh's scorching stare across the width of the room that separated them and she winced at J.J.'s reply, chancing a quick glance at Josh. His whole body had tensed and his expression was grim, his mouth thinned into a straight line, the black line of his brows lowered over eyes bleak with silent accusation as they met hers.

She looked back at J.J. and Murphy. The old horseman crooked one white eyebrow at her, his black eyes clearly inviting comment, but she refused to step near his conversational land mine.

She chose to ignore Murphy's question and J.J.'s cheerful response altogether.

"Both J.J. and I would love to take Caitlin back to Great Falls with us." She smiled at Caitlin. "But I'm not sure she wants to put up with my fashion advice and J.J.'s constant requests for stories."

"I love stories," J.J. chimed in. "And when Caitlin reads to me, she makes frog ribbits and bear growls."

Caitlin's face turned pink at the compliments and she shrugged with half-embarrassed pleasure. "Anybody can do that."

"Maybe," Murphy commented. "But not everyone thinks to do it. Might be you're a natural-born storyteller. Like me."

He winked at Caitlin and J.J., and they giggled.

"Will you finish the story you were telling us before Aunt Sarah came in?" Caitlin asked, her whole body leaning eagerly forward.

"Another time, perhaps," Sarah interjected. "We have errands to run before we go home, and it's getting late."

Despite protests by J.J. and Caitlin, Sarah smoothly bid them say goodbye and herded them toward the door.

"It was nice to meet you all," Murphy called after them. "You stop in again the next time you're here to visit your grandma and I'll finish the story."

"Okay." J.J.'s downcast face brightened and he flashed the two men a grin over his shoulder.

"Thank you. We will. It was nice to meet you, too, Murphy," Caitlin called, her dragging steps quickening.

"Goodbye, Murphy. Josh," Sarah managed to say without flinching when she met Josh's hard gaze. But she breathed a sigh of relief when they turned down the hall and she could no longer feel that piercing stare between her shoulder blades.

Visiting Murphy became a thrice-weekly highlight for J.J. and Caitlin after they dutifully paid a visit to their grandmother. Although they didn't see Josh again, as he rarely had time to visit until evening, they met Murphy's friend Jennifer Hightower and her three-year-old son, Wayne. Jennifer was married to Josh's brother, Lucas, and both she and Wayne clearly adored Murphy. The two little boys became fast friends, and Caitlin and Sarah were both warmly welcomed by Jennifer.

Several days had gone by and Sarah saw Josh only at a distance. The children raced off to the barn each afternoon when she brought them home from Molly's, and didn't return until she rang the dinner bell. J.J. chattered nonstop about Josh, Zach and the horses. Caitlin was less talkative, but she'd lost the dark circles under her eyes and her skin glowed healthy and alive. A certain air of peace had replaced the turmoil in her eyes and the edge of aggressive defensiveness that was so much a part of her personality had gradually eased since her arrival in Montana.

The children were clearly thriving; Sarah was not. She spent her days dealing with Patricia, who was slowly regaining her strength and growing more difficult and impatient. She was spending her nights tossing and turning, wrestling with whether or not to allow J.J. to have his blood tested. Her conscience told her she owed Josh that much, but she dreaded the possibility of a negative result. She could see only two alternatives: to allow the testing, or to tell Josh the entire truth. Neither was a good choice, but if Sarah told the truth, she feared that Josh would react as her mother had, and look at her with accusation and disgust. He also might *demand* testing and remove the decision from her control.

She was cleaning house and no closer to a decision early one afternoon when Molly and Wes pulled up in front of her gate.

"Hey, lady!" Wes swung his bulk out of the pickup. "What are you doing working inside on a day like this?"

Sarah took the hall throw rugs she'd been shaking out and tossed them over the porch railing, then walked to the top of the steps. "Isn't it a beautiful day?" She shaded her eyes with one hand and laughed down at him as he held the gate open for Molly and winked at her before they started up the walk toward her. "The rain shower we had this morning settled the dust."

"Thank goodness," Molly said with feeling. "But it's still too hot. We haven't had enough rain this month, and the wheat crop needs more than a little shower."

A shout of laughter drifted from the barn, and both Molly and Wes turned to investigate. J.J. was clearly visible sitting on the top rail of the corral, while inside, Caitlin rode in circles on a brown horse.

"What's going on?" Wes asked. "Are the kids having their riding lesson?"

"Yes," Sarah answered, watching J.J. throw back his head and laugh.

"Those kids are sure crazy about horses. It's hard to get them to talk about anything else," Wes commented.

Another shriek of laughter reached them, and Molly started back toward the gate.

"Come on, you two, I want to see what they're doing." She shoved open the gate and held it, waiting expectantly.

"You have to go with us, Sarah," Wes said as he ambled down the walkway toward his wife. "I've been wanting to see that boy of yours on a horse."

Sarah had planned to keep as much distance as possible between herself and Josh, but it wasn't likely that he would press her for an answer about J.J. in front of Wes and Molly. She grabbed her sunglasses, left the porch and joined her aunt and uncle.

"Relax in the saddle seat, but keep your back straight. Don't slouch." Josh stood just inside the corral, hands propped on his hips while he watched Caitlin canter Tornado in a circle.

"Afternoon, Josh." Wes leaned his forearms on a rail of the corral while Molly and Sarah elected to climb the rails and join J.J.

Josh glanced behind him just in time to see Sarah swing her bare, tanned legs over the top rail of the corral and sit down beside J.J. The hot sun gleamed off her silver-blond hair, the dark lenses of sunglasses concealing her eyes. Molly Hildebrandt joined her, taking a seat on the far side of J.J.

"Afternoon, Wes." Josh left his post and strolled across the dusty corral.

Wes nodded his head toward Caitlin. "The kids told us you were teaching them to ride. How are they doing?"

"Not bad." Josh leaned one shoulder against an upright post and glanced back at Caitlin. "To tell you the truth, I think she's a natural. It's a shame she lives in an apartment in the city and can't have a horse of her own."

Wes glanced to his left where J.J. was chattering excitedly to his mother.

"I think Sarah's trying to change that," he commented, his voice dropping to reach only Josh's ears. "She wants to keep Caitlin here, and Molly and I agree with her. Living in Los Angeles with Margaret and her string of boyfriends is the last place that little girl should be."

Josh nodded noncommittally. A short few days before, he'd had no tolerance for Caitlin's sometimes gutter language, zero patience with her belligerence, couldn't stand the silver studs in her quadruple-pierced ears, and wasn't sure he liked the fact that J.J. idolized her. More often than not, he'd thought she was an impossible brat. But working with her and watching her loving patience with J.J. had altered and softened his opinion. Besides, he strongly believed that no child deserved to be punched in the face by her mother's current boyfriend, nor that any child should grow up with the lack of nurturing and supervision that Caitlin had clearly experienced.

"I have to agree that no kid deserves a mother like Margaret," he said reluctantly. "And I've got to admire Caitlin's guts. I don't know many adults who would hitchhike from California to Montana, let alone a twelve-year-old girl."

"Damn near gave me a heart attack when I heard she'd done that," Wes said with feeling. "We're lucky nothing bad happened to her."

"Sounds to me like the worst happened before she left home in L.A.," Josh said dryly.

"Josh!"

Caitlin's call drew Josh's attention and he pushed away from the post. "Yeah?"

"Can J.J. get up behind me so we can show Uncle Wes and Aunt Molly how we ride double?"

"All right." Josh turned just in time to catch J.J. as he jumped straight off the top rail and into his arms. Josh's breath left his chest in an audible whoosh, and he staggered backward three steps before he regained his balance. "Hey, killer." He shifted J.J. back and looked down at him. "Next time wait until I'm set."

Sarah gasped when J.J. plummeted headlong away from the railing. But Josh's quick reflexes proved J.J.'s faith wasn't misplaced; he wrapped his short legs as far as they would go around Josh's lean waist and clutched fistfuls of Josh's cotton shirt.

The sunny smile J.J. gave Josh was returned, the stern lines of Josh's face relaxing into a warm grin.

The trust implicit in J.J.'s smile and the easy loving acceptance in Josh's caught at Sarah's heart; unaware she did so, she pressed her palm to the sharp ache just above her left breast.

Molly glanced at her, saw the gesture and the anguish in Sarah's expression, and looked back at Josh. But he and J.J. were walking away, crossing the corral to Tornado and Caitlin.

"Here you go, sport." Josh lifted J.J. onto the saddle behind Caitlin and waited until the boy clutched her around the waist in a hug that threatened to squeeze her in two. "Ease up a little, J.J. Let your cousin breathe. Good. Okay, Caitlin, he's all yours."

She flashed him a look of appreciation mingled with pride and wary reserve before she lifted the reins and kneed Tornado into a slow walk.

Josh knew exactly how she felt. The two of them had reached a truce of sorts; she was an apt, attentive pupil who clearly loved riding and took his instructions seriously. However, she was obviously still suspicious of his intentions toward Sarah, and he was just as suspicious of her newfound determination to stop swearing and of her obvious influence over J.J.

He strolled back across the dusty corral to join Wes. The women clapped and cheered encouragingly as Caitlin guided Tornado around the perimeter of the corral in a sedate walk, J.J. crowing proudly from his seat behind her.

The men discussed the weather and wheat prices for nearly fifteen minutes before Wes took off his Stetson and wiped the sweat from his brow.

"Whew, it's gettin' too hot to stand in the sun." He reached up and covered Molly's bare knee with one big hand. "What do you say we go up to the house, sit in the shade on the porch and have something cold to drink?"

Molly fanned her flushed face with one hand and agreed. "Is that okay with you, Sarah?"

"Absolutely," Sarah said promptly. "I made a pitcher of iced tea this morning."

"Great!" Wes settled his Stetson back over his brow and clapped Josh on the shoulder. "Sounds good, doesn't it, Josh?"

Josh stiffened and glanced at Sarah; her eyes and her expression were hidden behind the protection of dark lenses, but her slim body was subtly more tense. "Anything cold sounds good, Wes, but I think I'll pass. I'll unsaddle Tornado and turn him out so the kids can go up to the house with you." He caught up with Tornado, then reached up and swung J.J. down from behind the saddle before he took the reins from Caitlin. She grabbed the horn and stepped down as easily as if she'd been dismounting for years. Both children crawled between the bottom two corral rails and joined Sarah and Molly.

"I'll help," Wes said promptly. "Molly, Josh and I will be up to the house shortly. Save me some

ice!'' he shouted after her in an afterthought when
the two women and children were several yards
away.

"You better hurry," his wife threatened with a
laugh. "Tea with ice is sounding better and better
by the minute."

"Ten minutes," Wes called before he turned
back to Josh. "Now, son, let's get this horse put
away."

Josh gave in. He'd known Wes Hildebrandt for
more than thirty years and knew when the old
rancher was immovable. This was clearly one of
those times.

It was closer to twenty minutes before the men
joined the women on the porch.

"I thought you said you'd be here in ten
minutes?" Molly teased, greeting Wes with a tall
glass of ice-cold tea.

Wes paused to half drain the glass before answering. "Whew, that tastes good!" He took off
his Stetson and dropped into a rocker, settling his
hat on the bare porch boards beside his chair. "It
must be ninety degrees out there."

Sarah rose and crossed the porch to read the
numbers painted on the outdoor thermometer nailed
up beside the window. "Not quite—but close, Uncle Wes. It's eighty-eight."

"That's in the shade, Sarah," he corrected. "So
it's probably higher than ninety in that corral." He
waved his glass at J.J. and Caitlin, who were seated

on two chairs pushed up to a small wicker patio table on his left. "I hope you two appreciate the time Josh is taking to give you riding lessons. He could be inside with the air-conditioning turned on, you know."

J.J. giggled. "We don't have air-conditionin', Uncle Wes."

Ice tinkled against ice in the pitcher as Sarah poured another tall glass of tea and carried it to Josh. He'd taken a seat on the porch railing on the perimeter of the circle, his long legs stretched out in front of him, booted feet crossed at the ankles.

"Thanks," he said, still unable to read her expression behind her sunglasses.

"You're welcome," she answered politely before returning to her chair at the table next to Wes's rocker.

"I wish we had a horse like Tornado, Mommy." J.J. swung his legs energetically under the table, a fat ginger cookie clutched in one hand. "Or wild mustangs like Murphy used to catch and break."

"I wish we could catch wild horses." Caitlin's voice held wistful longing. "But there aren't any left."

"Maybe not real ones," Wes said, "but I've got the closest thing to wild horses as you're likely to get."

"Really?" Caitlin and J.J. chorused.

"Yup." Wes's shrewd blue gaze went from one rapt face to the other and he grinned expansively.

"To tell you the truth, I don't know how many I've got. I started out with fifty."

"Where are they?" Caitlin asked. "How did you get them?"

"Can we go see them? Can we ride them?" J.J. interrupted.

"Whoa, one question at a time." Wes chuckled and leaned forward, resting his elbows on his knees. "It all started about fifteen years ago. I had around fifty head of prime horseflesh, but the market was terrible—so low that I couldn't sell them for anywhere near as much as it had cost me to raise them. I was disgusted. I'd sold off a lot of cattle that year and had more pasture than I needed, so I decided to turn the horses out to pasture and hold on to them for a few years until the market improved."

"But that was fifteen years ago," Josh put in dryly. "And they're still there."

"Wow," Caitlin said in awe. "Why did you leave them there?"

Wes shrugged. "Several years went by before the market started moving upward, but by then those horses were as wild as March hares. I'm getting too old to catch and break rough stock."

Molly chuckled. "Besides, he likes the idea of horses living wild and untouched out there on those two thousand acres."

"I don't know about the untouched part," Josh drawled. "In my younger, wilder days, Lucas, Zach and I used to sneak out there and rope and try to ride them.''

"The hell you say," Wes exploded, eyeing the younger man with chagrin.

"Yeah." Josh grinned unrepentantly. "I had a few cracked ribs from those horses of yours, Wes."

"You're a better cowboy than I thought you were if you managed to get a rope on any of them," Wes commented. "Let alone ride one."

"It took three of us to do it," Josh recalled. "And I'm not saying any of us managed to stay on for the whole eight seconds. I remember eating dirt, and I don't recall that Lucas or Zach did any better."

"Did you ever see Uncle Wes's wild horses, Mommy?" J.J. asked.

"Sure she did." Wes leaned over and slipped an arm around Sarah's shoulders and hugged her affectionately. "I took her out there every chance I got—which was whenever I could kidnap her away from her mother in town. She loved the horses, didn't you, honey?"

"Yes, I did." Sarah tensed and endured the suffocation that threatened the moment Wes caught her shoulder in an affectionate light hug. Still, the sensation grew swiftly until she could barely breathe. "I was crazy about those horses." She stood, and Wes's arm slipped from her shoulder. Carefully she sucked air into her starving lungs and managed a smile. "I'm going to get some more ice cubes from the kitchen. Does anyone else want anything?"

"More cookies, Mommy," J.J. answered promptly, unaware that anything was wrong. "The plate's empty."

Sarah pulled open the screen door. "I suspect the plate's empty because a certain little boy ate them all."

"Where is the pasture, Uncle Wes?" Caitlin asked with intense curiosity.

Josh had grown to know Caitlin over the past two weeks and would have been alerted by the focused intensity on her face as she questioned her great-uncle, but he was distracted by Sarah. He remembered that Sarah had adored the big, bluff rancher, and he was puzzled by her uncomfortable withdrawal from his affectionate hug. From his vantage point slightly outside the haphazard circle of chairs grouped around the table, Josh hadn't missed the quickly hidden concern on Molly's open face when she watched Sarah slip out from under Wes's arm.

Not only had Sarah's face seemed paler, but she'd also appeared to be having trouble catching her breath.

It didn't make sense. Josh frowned, his gaze drifting over Wes as he waved his hand toward the north while he told Caitlin and J.J. where the horses raced free. Then Josh's gaze moved on, and his eyes narrowed as he registered the full pitcher of cold tea and the dozen or so ice cubes that floated in the pale brew.

Sarah didn't go to the kitchen because she wanted ice. What the hell is going on?

Chapter Six

Sarah was standing at the counter, taking cookies from a tin container and arranging them on a plate, when someone entered the kitchen. She glanced over her shoulder, expecting to see Molly, and found Josh.

Josh saw her slim body tense and her features smooth into impassiveness.

"Are you all right?" he asked bluntly. She stared at him with dark, fathomless eyes for a long, silent moment.

"What do you mean?" she said finally.

"You turned pale as a ghost out there." Josh gestured toward the porch with the hand holding his nearly empty tea glass. "And it looked like you were having trouble breathing. Are you sick?"

"No." Sarah turned her back to him and replaced the lid on the cookie tin. "No, I'm not sick."

"Then what's wrong with you?"

Sarah drew a deep breath and turned to face him. "Nothing. I must have gotten too much sun. I felt faint for a moment, that's all." He frowned at her, clearly unconvinced. "Do you want your glass refilled?"

"Sure." Josh didn't believe her. Something had happened out there on the porch, and he didn't think it was caused by the heat. She clearly didn't want to tell him, however, so he let her fill his glass and then followed her back to the porch.

To Sarah's relief, no one but Josh seemed to have noticed her reaction to Wes's hug. Caitlin and J.J. were pumping Wes for more details about the herd of wild horses and barely looked up when she set the plate of cookies on the table in front of them and took a seat in the porch swing.

Two weeks later, the house was still. Sarah carefully eased open J.J.'s bedroom door and peeked inside. J.J. lay sprawled facedown on the bed, his favorite stuffed animal, Tigger, clutched under one arm. Sarah tiptoed across the room and drew the shade, shadowing the room from the hot afternoon sun outside.

She paused across the hall to look in on Caitlin

and found her asleep, too, the shades already drawn against the sun.

Sarah didn't know why both Caitlin and J.J. had decided to take a nap on this hot Sunday afternoon. She only knew she was thankful that they had. Given the amount of time she spent twisting and turning at night, her own lack of sleep was catching up to her.

She stifled a yawn as she entered her own bedroom and within minutes had pulled the shades, shed her sandals and sundress, and stretched out atop the bedspread.

Sarah didn't realize the children were missing until nearly three hours later.

She'd checked their bedrooms when she woke from her nap, and when she found their beds empty, assumed that they'd awakened earlier and gone to play at the barn. However, after an hour elapsed and they didn't return, she began to worry. A bank of clouds had rolled in, obscuring the sun and chilling the afternoon air. The forecast was for rain, wind and possible hail; Sarah wanted J.J. and Caitlin tucked safely inside the protection of the house before the storm arrived. She shed her sundress for jeans, a long-sleeved cotton shirt and boots and hurried outside.

She stood on the porch and called their names, but there was no response. She walked around the house to check the tent J.J. had erected with Caitlin the day before, but the canvas shelter was empty.

A search of the big barn with its attached corral and sheds was equally fruitless. The sound of a truck engine reached her just as she exited the wide doors.

"Josh!" Truly worried now, Sarah ran toward the slowing truck, waving her arms.

"What's wrong?" Josh braked and was outside the pickup, striding toward her, before she could reach him.

"It's J.J. and Caitlin." A gust of wind caught her hair, whisking it across her face, and she pushed the pale strands out of her eyes. "They're not in the house or the yard. I've looked in the sheds and barn—I can't find them anywhere."

His glance went past her to the open barn door. "You're sure they're not in the barn? Did you look in the hayloft?"

"No, I called, but they didn't answer."

"I'll climb up and look. One of the barn cats has a litter of half-grown kittens in the corner of the loft. Maybe the kids were playing with them and didn't hear you."

"I hope you're right." Sarah looked up at the sky. "The weather forecast is for rain and possibly hail. I don't want them out in this."

"Don't worry, we'll find them." Josh caught her arm and turned her toward the barn, slowing his long strides so she could keep up with him. "They can't have gone far."

But the children weren't in the loft. Nor were they playing in the shaded green interior of the grove of trees and brush near the spring.

"Josh, where can they be?"

Sarah's blue eyes were alive with worry, her face tense with anxiety. Josh wanted to pull her close and soothe her, but he forcibly restrained himself. She wouldn't welcome the gesture, and he didn't need the pain her rejection would bring.

"We'll find them," he said grimly. The wind caught at the brim of his Stetson and he anchored it with his hand, glancing up at the threatening sky. "I've got to get a couple of pregnant mares into the barn. Why don't you check their rooms once more? Maybe they left a note."

"All right." Sarah cast a worried look at the darkening sky and hurried toward the house.

It wasn't until Josh was closing the stall door on the second of the mares that he noticed Tornado was missing. A swift check of the tack room confirmed that the saddle and bridle he'd been using on the gelding for J.J.'s and Caitlin's riding lessons were missing, too.

Hands on hips, he stared at the empty stall for a long moment. Not only was Tornado gone, but so was Rum.

"Rum's never very far away from those kids,"

he muttered aloud. "Wherever the dog is, that's where they are."

But where was Rum?

Josh strode to the open barn door and looked out. The sky was growing darker by the minute; even as he watched, lightning arced and cracked, followed by the deep boom of thunder. In the barn behind him, Baby whinnied, the sound a trumpeting challenge to nature's tempest.

Josh stiffened, the stallion's call reminding him of Caitlin's fascination with horses, and the dozens of questions she'd asked Wes about his wild band.

"Damn." He knew exactly where Caitlin and J.J. had gone. He spun and reentered the barn, collecting a blanket, saddle and bridle from the tack room before entering Baby's stall.

"What are you doing?"

Josh barely glanced up when Sarah entered the barn. "I'm going after the kids."

"You are?" Confused, Sarah watched the swift movements of his hands as he smoothed the saddle blanket over Baby's back and swung the saddle atop it. "Where are they?"

"Tornado's missing—and so is Rum. I think the kids went to Wes's pasture to see the horses."

"Oh, no!" Sarah darted a glance over her shoulder at the open barn door where the wind was gusting, carrying dust and dry leaves. "Are you sure?"

"No." Josh yanked the girth tight and buckled it snugly against Baby's belly. "But I remember the look on Caitlin's face when Wes was telling her about that herd of wild horses. Add to that the fact that both Tornado and Rum are gone—and J.J.—and I think it's a pretty fair bet that they've gone looking for your uncle's wild bunch. I'm going after them.''

"On Baby? Why don't you take the truck. Wouldn't it be faster?''

"Not where I'm going. It's faster if I cut straight across the pasture.'' He didn't add that it would be easier to quarter the land on horseback than from a truck seat, in case J.J. or Caitlin was lying injured somewhere.

"I'm going with you.''

"No, you're not.'' Josh found himself talking to empty air. Sarah had disappeared into the tack room, quickly reappearing lugging a saddle, blanket and bridle. "Stay here,'' he ordered as he slipped the latch and led Baby from his stall. "If I'm wrong and they come home, you'll be here for them.''

"No.'' Sarah was busy slipping the bit between the teeth of Zach's saddle horse, a glossy bay mare, in the stall next to Baby. "I think you're right—the kids have gone looking for Uncle Wes's wild horses. They've talked of nothing else ever since they heard that story. They've pestered Uncle Wes to take them out to the pasture, but for one reason or another, he hasn't found time.'' She tossed the saddle blanket over the mare's back and smoothed the wrinkles away. "I should have guessed something was up when Caitlin wanted to take a nap this afternoon.''

Josh wrapped Baby's reins around a post, stepped into the stall and hefted the saddle, swinging it onto the mare's back. "How long has it been since you've done any riding?" he asked abruptly, making short work of straps and buckles.

"A long time," she answered just as abruptly. "But I'll keep up. If I don't, leave me behind. I know the way. I won't get lost."

Josh frowned down into her determined face. "You've got a lot in common with that stubborn niece of yours," he commented brusquely.

Sarah didn't respond. He shoved the reins into her hand and left the stall to get Baby. He stopped by the tack room, walked inside and returned with slickers, one of which he tossed to Sarah. "You better put it on," he ordered.

Sarah followed Josh out of the barn and mounted, urging the mare into motion. Josh was shrugging into the horseman's split-backed rain slicker as he rode and she followed suit, casting a worried glance at the ominous black sky.

Baby galloped in the lead, the bay mare close behind. So close was the mare that Sarah was almost unseated when the stallion came to an abrupt halt, the mare skidding to a stop behind him.

"What? What is it?" Sarah demanded frantically, clutching the saddle horn.

"Tornado," Josh said succinctly, and urged Baby into a fast lope.

He was leaning from the saddle to catch the gelding's bridle by the time Sarah arrived. She reined the mare in a half circle around the gelding, but saw no sign of injury.

"Did he throw them? What happened?"

"The reins are wrapped around the saddle horn," Josh told her. "At a guess, I'd say they got off on their own and forgot to ground hitch him. He might have walked off and left them."

"Great," Sarah groaned. "Just great. That means they're on foot." She twisted in the saddle, scanning the horizon, but found no movement. "They could be anywhere!"

Josh was silent, his gaze continuing a rapid search of the gelding. His eyes narrowed over the horse's hooves and fetlocks and he whistled softly.

"Did you find something?" Sarah asked sharply.

"Clay dust on his hooves." Josh released Tornado's bridle and slapped him on his hindquarters. "Go home, boy." The horse jumped and ran a few steps before slowing to a walk, continuing along the cattle track in the direction of the Rocking D. Josh gestured to Sarah to follow Baby, and started the stallion down the dirt path in the opposite direction. "This track leads across Drummond land to Wes's north pasture and his horse herd. A lot of clay cliffs and coulee bottoms lie along this track. I'm betting Tornado left the kids and has been following the track home.'' He lifted Baby into a fast lope.

The wind picked up, whipping Sarah's hair across her face; she narrowed her eyes against the tangling strands and crouched lower in the saddle, urging the mare faster. Baby's ebony coat was a dark blur in front of her.

"There they are!" Josh shouted over his shoulder, and kicked the big stallion into a run.

"Oh, thank God!" She urged the mare on, following Josh as he raced down the track.

Ahead of them, Caitlin and J.J. stopped walking, their relief underlaid with trepidation as the horses drew up beside them.

"Are you hurt?" Josh demanded, swiftly skimming their guilty faces.

"No," Caitlin responded. "We're fine."

Satisfied, Josh flicked a glance at the sky and stepped out of the saddle. He caught J.J. under the arms and tossed him into Baby's saddle. "Hold on," he ordered. He grabbed Caitlin and lifted her up behind Sarah. "All hell's about to break loose, Sarah. If we're lucky, we'll make it to shelter," he shouted as he remounted with swift ease, one arm holding J.J. securely against his midriff while the other hand gathered up the reins. He leaned forward and sent Baby racing across the rough pastureland toward the crumbling rock of a nearby butte.

Sarah grabbed one of Caitlin's hands and pulled

it around her waist to anchor the girl before she kicked the mare in the ribs and chased after Josh.

Above them, lightning cracked, and thunder rolled in a deep-throated, threatening rumble that shook the ground beneath the horses' hooves.

"Please, God," she prayed fervently. "Don't let her step in a gopher hole."

The mare couldn't keep up with the fast quarter horse stud, but before Baby could leave Sarah and the mare too far behind, Josh stopped him. He dismounted and pulled J.J. after him, grabbing Caitlin and swinging her to the ground before Sarah was out of the saddle. He caught Sarah's arm and urged her toward a wide shelf of rock where a small, sheltered cave was created by the shelf above and a thick chunk of black rock leaning at right angles against it.

"Crawl inside and sit with your back against the rock. Put Caitlin on your lap," Josh ordered.

Sarah dropped to all fours and scrambled inside, stretching out her legs in front of her just as Caitlin clambered in beside her and onto her lap.

Thunder rumbled, shaking the ground beneath them as Josh slid his long legs in beside Sarah's, one arm snagging J.J. around the waist and pulling him under shelter and onto his lap just as the heavens opened and hail pelted down.

The noise was deafening. Caitlin and J.J. covered their ears and huddled close.

"Josh? Where's Rum?" J.J. twisted to look up at Josh.

The little boy's eyes were huge green saucers, his face pale with fright. Josh had to bend his head close to hear his shouted words, so great was the roar of the hail and thunder outside. He caught J.J.'s chin in his hand and turned his head sideways to speak close to his ear. "He's safe. Look at our feet."

J.J. did as he was bid. Squeezed into the narrow area where the slanted black rock met the gravelly ground, his black coat barely visible in the gloomy darkness of the tiny cave, lay Rum. The dog panted, breathing heavily from the hard run to shelter.

Josh felt the little boy relax and J.J.'s hands loosed their punishing grip on his arm where it wrapped around his small waist.

A scant two feet from his right side, hail slammed onto the ground, white pellets bouncing to ping against the yellow slicker that protected his legs.

As swiftly as it had started, the hail ceased. And the rain started. The skies opened and released rain that poured down in torrents, replacing the hail with water that splashed close, dampening Josh's legs and right side through the opening of the three-sided shelter.

He turned his head, swiftly assessing Sarah and Caitlin's features, both pale in the dim light. "Everyone okay?"

Caitlin nodded solemnly, her eyes wide and frightened.

"Yes," Sarah said.

"Good." He nodded and turned his head to look out at the storm. Outside the shelter, Baby and the bay mare stood guard, their heads bowed against the lashing downpour of rain, their tails turned into the driving wind.

Sarah, too, watched the storm, but her gaze was continually drawn back to Josh's profile. Etched against the faint light outside, the bone structure of his face was sculpted and strong, with high cheekbones and a straight nose, stubborn jawline and firm lips.

Inside the low-ceilinged enclosure, weighted down by the children in their laps, their bodies were locked together, shoulder, hip, thigh and leg, but strangely enough, Sarah didn't panic. Instead of her feeling threatened by the contact, Josh's warm, hard body pressed firmly against her side made her feel protected and safe.

She sat perfectly still for long moments, trying to absorb the bewildering, unexpected reaction of her body to his. His gaze left the downpour outside, his chin dropping to brush against the down-soft blond hair on the crown of J.J.'s head. He glanced sideways, trapping Sarah's gaze with his, and she shivered, her body heating deep inside at the dark intensity of his stare.

"Is Baby safe outside?" Caitlin's subdued voice was edged with worry.

Sarah tore her gaze from Josh and glanced down at the twelve-year-old's bowed head. "Yes, I think so." She looked back at Josh. "The horses weren't harmed by the hail, were they?"

"No, I don't think so." He fixed Caitlin with a stern look. "But you kids could have been—and so could Rum. What were you doing this far from home?"

"We were going to visit Uncle Wes's wild horses," Caitlin responded. "But J.J. had to go to the bathroom and when we got off Tornado, he ran away."

"I'm sorry, Josh." J.J. twisted around to look up into Josh's face. "Caitlin told me to go before we left home—but I didn't need to then."

Sarah stifled a laugh and saw Josh's lips quiver before his mouth firmed into a hard line once more. Her gaze met his over the top of the children's heads, and they shared silent laughter in a rare moment of complete understanding.

"Yes, well..." Josh cleared his throat, hiding a chuckle behind a cough. "That's not the point, J.J. The real issue here is that you kids didn't tell your mother where you were going before you left home. Not only did you scare her, but if anything had happened to you, it might have been hours before we found you."

"I'm sorry." J.J.'s bottom lip quivered. "And I'm sorry, Mommy."

"It's not J.J.'s fault," Caitlin said. "It's mine. I wanted to visit Uncle Wes's wild horses and he didn't have time to take us. I thought we'd be back in an hour or two and Aunt Sarah would never know." She bent her head, her long ebony braid falling forward over her shoulder. "I'm sorry, Aunt Sarah," she mumbled. "I didn't mean to make you worry."

Sarah smoothed her palm down the mussed braid and patted Caitlin's shoulder. "Just don't disappear like this again, Caitlin. If you'd told me you wanted to go visit the horses, I would have taken you."

"But you're always busy at the hospital with Grandmother Patricia," she protested. "I didn't want to bother you."

A stab of guilt pierced Sarah. Was she too busy, spread too thin? Was she neglecting Caitlin and J.J.?

"You wouldn't have been bothering me, Caitlin," Sarah reassured her. "I would have found time to take you."

Josh read the swift expression of worry and guilt that flitted across Sarah's face. Dammit, who did she think she was, Superwoman? The kid was right; Sarah was doing too much. "Next time, ask me," he said gruffly. "I'll take you."

Sarah's gaze raced to meet his, and she found

him frowning at her, an emotion she couldn't read darkening his eyes.

"The kid's right," he declared abruptly. "You're doing too much already. I'll take them to see Wes's horses."

Chapter Seven

Overwhelmed by his offer and the ability to read her feelings that precipitated it, Sarah could only nod in agreement.

Josh felt as if he were drowning in her eyes, where gratitude swirled with something deeper, darker.

"Will you really, Josh?"

J.J.'s voice claimed his attention, and Josh tore his gaze from Sarah's to look down at the little boy.

"Yeah, I really will." He fixed the little boy with a stern look before moving to include Caitlin. "But that doesn't mean you're not going to get punished for running off today without telling your mother where you were going and asking for permission."

"Uh-oh." J.J. tucked his chin against his chest and glanced sideways at his mother.

The trepidation on his face was echoed on Caitlin's features when she twisted to look up into Sarah's face. "I really am sorry that we worried you, Aunt Sarah, and I'm ready to take my punishment."

Sarah felt the twelve-year-old's slight body tense, as if the child expected a blow. Sarah's first impulse was to pull her close and reassure her, but she stifled the instinct.

"What the two of you did could have had grave consequences," she said instead. "And I agree with Josh, your actions require discipline. Therefore, I'm grounding you for a week. That means no television, no movie this weekend and no riding lessons."

J.J. opened his mouth to object, but quickly snapped it shut when Caitlin glared warningly at him.

"And you have to replace the time you would have spent during your riding lessons doing chores for Josh—whatever he decides to assign you—to repay him for the time he spent and the trouble he went to to find you today," Sarah continued firmly. "If that's all right with him," she added.

Josh felt a surge of pleasure that Sarah had included him in what was clearly a wielding of parental authority within her family circle. He had little time to savor the unfamiliar feeling, however, for two sets of solemn eyes switched from Sarah's face to his.

"Is it, Josh?" J.J. asked.

Josh nodded slowly. "Yeah," he said, his deep voice a judicious drawl. "I guess so."

Caitlin let out the breath she'd been holding. "Is that it?" she asked, her gaze flicking between the two adults. "That's the punishment?"

"Yes." Sarah looked back at her, meeting Caitlin's disbelief with straightforward seriousness. "I think sentencing you to additional chores and taking away your privileges for a week is punishment enough."

Caitlin's green eyes darkened, her gaze shifting to search Josh's face before returning to Sarah.

She drew a deep breath, her chin firming with resolve. "All right. We won't ever leave again without checking with you first."

Outside the enclosure, the rain slowed and then stopped. Josh lifted J.J. off his lap and set him on his feet outside before crawling out himself. He bent to look back into the tiny cave.

"Rum, out."

The big dog inched out from beneath the narrow overhang, lunging to his feet outside and shaking himself before sniffing the rain-clean air.

"You're next, Caitlin." Josh held out his hand, and the twelve-year-old caught it, allowing him to tug her into the open air.

Wordlessly Josh turned back and held out his

hand once more. Sarah's palm met his, his callused fingers and palm closing with easy strength around her much smaller hand. He supported her as she inched her way out of the rock-walled lean-to, pulling her easily to her feet.

The ground was drenched and her boots slipped on wet rock, sending her staggering into Josh. He caught her, one hand holding hers tightly against his chest, while the other arm instinctively wrapped around her shoulder to brace her safely against his solid bulk.

Startled, Sarah stared up into his face. Even through the jeans, shirts and heavy slickers that separated them, her body was achingly aware of the hard male angles she pressed against. His thick lashes half lowered in an effort to conceal the quick heat that leapt in his eyes, while his pulse throbbed swiftly at the base of his throat. Inches from her lips, black stubble shadowed his jawline. When they were dating, Sarah remembered with sudden, vivid clarity, he'd had to shave twice daily to keep from marking her sensitive skin.

As quickly as he'd caught her, Josh released her, his hands moving to her shoulders to set her away from him. She staggered from the suddenness of movement, caught herself and quickly stepped backward and out from under his grasp. He turned away from her, his face set in stern, uncompromising lines, and moved to the horses.

"The saddles are soaked," he said over his

shoulder, bending to run a hand over Baby's left front leg. He ducked under the big stallion's neck and continued his inspection on the far side, his voice carrying easily to the three watching him as he crooned softly to the horse. He ran an assessing eye over Baby, then did the same with Zach's mare. "They're fine," he pronounced at last. "A few bruises from the hail, but no serious damage." He caught J.J. around the waist and swung him up into Baby's saddle. "Caitlin, you'll have to ride behind Sarah." He waited until Sarah had mounted before giving Caitlin a boost up.

Caitlin grimaced as dampness from the drenched mare's coat soaked through her jeans. "Yuk. She's all wet!"

"You'll be wet, too, by the time we get home," Josh said.

Never humble for long, Caitlin turned, and her green eyes shot sparks as she glowered at him. He responded with a swift, teasing grin.

Josh turned away, swung into the saddle behind J.J., and led the way toward home, hot baths and dry clothes.

As they neared the Rocking D, he found himself increasingly torn by his conflicting feelings for Sarah. The anger and sense of betrayal was still strong, but so was the undeniable depth of feeling that wouldn't let go of his heart. He stubbornly refused to admit to himself that any possibility existed that he still loved her; instead, he wrote it off

as lust and grimly swore to ignore his hormones
and avoid Sarah.

Several days later at high noon, the thermometer
hit ninety-three degrees. Sarah held the door to
Connie's Cafe open while J.J. bounced past her,
followed by Caitlin, before she stepped into the
blessedly cool, air-conditioned interior herself. The
popular cafe was busy with the lunchtime crowd.
Each red-vinyl-covered stool at the counter was occupied; wheat farmers from outlying farms perched
next to office workers in summer dresses. Young
mothers and their children, dressed in bright summer shorts and sandals, filled two of the booths; an
elderly couple drank iced tea in another; and two
more booths held single occupants with all but the
crowns of their heads concealed by the high-backed
booths. A crew of cowboys in dusty boots and jeans
had their hats hung on hooks beside the last three
booths at the back of the restaurant.

Sarah scanned the cafe but couldn't find a single
vacant seat.

J.J. tugged impatiently on her hand. "Mommy,
I'm starvin'."

"I know, kiddo," she answered, smiling sympathetically as he rubbed his stomach and grimaced
dramatically. "But it doesn't look like there's any
place for us to sit."

J.J. groaned and shifted from foot to foot, his
green gaze inspecting the occupants of the cafe.

"Hey." He brightened and pulled his hand from Sarah's. "There's Josh! We can sit with him."

"No—wait, J.J...." Sarah's quick grab for his hand was too late. The little boy darted around a waitress juggling three steaming plates, and between two white-haired men in shirtsleeves, to climb up onto the bench of a booth with only one occupant halfway to the rear of the cafe.

J.J. chattered, pointing toward the door, and the man sitting with his broad back to Sarah twisted to look over his shoulder at her.

"I'm sorry, ma'am, but we don't have a table open."

The harried young waitress's words distracted Sarah, and she tore her gaze away from Josh's.

"We'll wait. How long do you think it will be?" she asked.

"Mommy!"

J.J.'s treble carried over the hum of voices and the clatter of crockery, down the length of the cafe to Sarah. The waitress turned to follow Sarah's gaze, and saw J.J. waving enthusiastically.

"There's room for us, Mommy!"

"Good." The waitress's face brightened and she flashed Sarah a relieved look. "I'll bring menus right away," she assured her before bustling off.

"Oh, but..." Sarah began, her voice trailing off as she realized that several women at nearby tables were watching with interest. Two of the women were members of Patricia's bridge club. Sarah nodded at them, forcing herself to smile pleasantly as she slipped an arm around Caitlin's shoulders and gently urged the twelve-year-old ahead of her toward the booth. "Come on, Caitlin. It seems J.J. has found seats for us."

Josh saw Sarah and Caitlin start toward him, and slipped out of the booth.

J.J. promptly scrambled off the opposite bench. "I get to sit with you," he declared as he ducked under Josh's arm to clamber up on the seat. He scooted across the bench to the far corner and smiled sunnily up at Josh.

"J.J., what are you doing?"

Sarah's voice drew Josh's attention from the little boy. He glanced around to find her and Caitlin standing next to the booth, their expressions equally doubtful.

Short of hauling J.J. out of the booth and telling them all to get lost, there was nothing Josh could do without causing a scene, especially since most of the occupants of the cafe were watching avidly. *So much for avoiding Sarah,* he thought.

"He's joining me for lunch," he said, gesturing abruptly toward the empty bench opposite J.J. "And so are you—have a seat."

"Are you sure?" Sarah hadn't missed his reluctance. "We can wait until another booth or table is empty if you'd rather not have company."

"No." Josh shook his head. "Sit down, Caitlin."

The girl obeyed him, sliding across the bench

seat to the far corner. Sarah hesitated, but the harried waitress chose that moment to appear at her elbow, and Sarah quickly joined Caitlin. The waitress slid vinyl-covered menus in front of all four and hurried off again.

"I want a cheeseburger with everything," J.J. announced firmly. "With extra pickles—lots of extra pickles."

Josh's grim humor evaporated and he couldn't stop the answering grin that lifted his mouth when he looked down at J.J.

"Oh, yeah?" he drawled, delighted and intrigued that the little boy's preference matched his. "Me, too." He lifted an eyebrow in inquiry. "How do you feel about chocolate milk shakes?"

J.J. beamed up at him. "They're my favorite."

"Good." Josh slapped his menu shut and glanced across the table at Sarah. "That takes care of the men. How about you two?"

Caught staring, Sarah dropped her gaze to her menu and chose the first item she read. "I think I'll have a turkey sandwich and iced tea."

"Caitlin?"

"I want a cheeseburger and a strawberry shake."

"Yuk!" J.J. grimaced. "Strawberry's disgusting."

Caitlin rolled her eyes and closed her menu, sliding it across the tabletop to Sarah.

Josh glanced over his shoulder and lifted a hand

to catch the waitress's attention. Busy though the cafe was, it wasn't long until they were served.

"This is the best cheeseburger ever," J.J. announced. A chocolate mustache decorated his upper lip.

"You say that about every cheeseburger you eat," Caitlin scoffed dismissingly, daintily sipping her own strawberry ice cream through a straw.

"Nuh-uh," the little boy protested.

"J.J.," Sarah said warningly, shaking her head at him when he turned a militant green gaze her way. "No arguing—eat your lunch."

He subsided, and Sarah turned her attention to the turkey-on-wheat sandwich that she'd been pretending to eat for the past twenty minutes. Fortunately, J.J. and Caitlin had plied Josh with questions, preventing what Sarah was sure would otherwise have been awkward silence. She was achingly aware of the man across the short width of the table.

The bell over the cafe's front door jingled and Caitlin looked up, breaking into a smile and waving at the entrants.

Sarah glanced past Josh's shoulder and found Jennifer Hightower and Trey Weber, Wayne perched on his shoulders, walking toward them.

"Hi, guys." Jennifer's smile lit her face and the hand she dropped to Josh's arm brought his gaze up to hers.

"Hey, Jen," he responded. He reached out and

caught one of Wayne's boots where his little foot rested against Trey's chest, waggling it and making the little boy giggle. "How you doin', slugger?"

"Fine, Unca Josh," he answered.

"You want to join us?" Josh asked Jennifer. "It might be a little crowded, but we can pull up a chair or two."

"Thanks, but we're meeting Annabel for lunch." She gestured toward a booth in the rear of the cafe, waving at the occupant before returning her attention to Josh and Sarah.

Sarah twisted, looking over her shoulder. The white-haired woman sitting in the booth smiled and waved and Sarah responded with a heartfelt smile of her own.

"I haven't seen Annabel Fitch since I got back," she commented. "I should have called her."

"You've had more important things on your mind than social calls, Sarah," Jennifer said sympathetically. "I'm sure Annabel understands. How is your mother?"

"Better," Sarah responded. "The doctors are increasingly optimistic that she'll make a full recovery."

"That's wonderful news."

"Mommy, I'm hungry," Wayne said, interrupting his mother.

Jennifer rolled her eyes and laughed, sharing a quick glance of understanding with Sarah. "I guess we better join Annabel and feed this starving child.'' She took a step away from the booth before halting. "I almost forgot—you're coming to Annabel's party, aren't you, Sarah?"

Confused, Sarah shook her head. "What party?"

"Her birthday party. She's turning sixty."

"We weren't invited...and I don't think—"

"It's a community party—nobody was officially invited," Jennifer said quickly. "A group of teachers from school got together and arranged it, then we took turns calling everybody in the county to tell them. We must have missed you because you're not listed in the phone book yet, but I'm officially inviting you. Will you come?"

"I don't know, Jennifer." Sarah stalled. "I'm not sure if we—"

"I won't take no for an answer," Jennifer interrupted firmly. "I'm sure you need a break from the hospital by now. The party starts at six o'clock next Saturday at the community center—and bring J.J. and Caitlin. It's a family party."

"Can we go, Mommy?" J.J. interjected excitedly.

"We'll see."

"You two talk her into it," Jennifer said to Caitlin. "It's going to be great fun."

"Want down, Trey," Wayne demanded, tugging fistfuls of blond hair.

Trey winced. "Ouch! Cut that out, Wayne." He lifted the little boy off his shoulders and set him on the floor, retaining a firm hold on his hand. "Come on, killer, let's go put some money in the jukebox."

"I wanna go, too!" J.J. declared immediately.

"You stay here, J.J.," Sarah said quickly. "Trey doesn't need two little boys to help him."

"I'll go with them," Caitlin told her, daintily wiping her mouth with her napkin. She waited patiently for Sarah to stand before slipping out of the booth to stand by Trey.

"Be good, Wayne," Jennifer admonished her son. "I'll see you later, Sarah—Josh. Don't forget, Sarah, Saturday at six." She waggled her fingers and left to join Annabel.

Sarah seated herself just as Josh slid out of the other side of the booth and let J.J. clamber across the seat to jump to the floor. The two little boys immediately put their heads together, whispering, before they ran, giggling, up the aisle toward the neon-lit jukebox, followed more slowly by Caitlin and Trey.

Sarah's worried gaze followed J.J. as he raced off with Wayne.

"He'll be fine." Josh's deep voice interrupted her thoughts. "Trey and Caitlin will keep an eye on him."

Her gaze left the little boys and flicked back to Josh.

"I'm sure they will." She sighed, absentmindedly swirling the straw in her glass of iced tea, setting the ice cubes tinkling. "I suppose I have to admit that I tend to be overprotective. It's one of the hazards of being a single parent.''

"You don't have to be a single parent," Josh said bluntly, his hard blue stare pinning hers. "I'm more than willing to shoulder my share of worry for my son."

"I believe you," she answered quietly, acknowledging aloud for the first time that she'd been wrong about Josh's view of fatherhood.

Josh drew a deep breath, profoundly affected by her simple, sincere words. "Then let me," he replied just as quietly.

"You want to have blood tests." She didn't need his nod of agreement to confirm her words.

Before he could answer, the jukebox came to life, filling the cafe with the music and lyrics from a song they'd often danced to when they were dating.

The words Josh had been about to utter froze on his tongue. Riveted by the awareness that leapt into her eyes, he could only stare back, trapped in memories.

Memories of moving slowly to the music, Sarah's arms wrapped around his neck, her mouth soft, hot and hungry beneath his, her soft curves pressed against the harder angles of his much bigger body until neither of them could wait any longer for him to be inside her, loving her.

Josh ruthlessly beat down the urge to lean across the table, grab Sarah and carry her off somewhere isolated where they could be alone—alone to replay any one of a dozen scenes from their past when they'd made love. He didn't want to admit that the time they'd spent together was unforgettable—and clearly not repeatable.

He ripped his gaze from hers and slid out of the booth.

"I have to get back to work," he said roughly. He lifted his Stetson from the brass hook and settled it on his head, nodded an abrupt goodbye and strode away from her down the aisle.

Sarah watched him go without a word, shaken by the seething cauldron of emotions that raged through her—even more shaken by the storm of memories visible in Josh's turquoise eyes.

He stopped at the cash register and handed folded bills to the waitress before pausing to speak briefly to Trey and the children. Then he disappeared through the cafe's front door.

Sarah drew a deep breath, only then realizing that she'd been scarcely breathing while she watched him. She glanced at the jukebox and saw Trey swing Wayne and J.J. off their feet, carrying a laughing little boy under each arm as he and Caitlin started toward her.

J.J. is thriving in Butte Creek, she thought, watching the delighted, ear-to-ear grin that lit his face—thriving under the care and affection he was receiving from Josh and the wide circle of family and friends that surrounded him.

He's at home here. The knowledge twisted her

heart. *How can I take him back to Great Falls? On the other hand,* she thought bleakly, *how can I stay here and share J.J. with Josh when it would mean seeing Josh nearly every day and knowing we have no future together?*

There were no answers for Sarah.

"Was Mrs. Fitch your schoolteacher, Aunt Sarah?" Caitlin asked, standing patiently while Sarah fashioned her hair in a French braid.

"No, she was the principal when I was in high school," Sarah replied. Her fingers moved deftly, weaving the intricate plait that started on the crown of Caitlin's head and ended with the long braid swinging free to the middle of her shoulder blades.

"Did you like her?" J.J. asked with interest. Ordered not to get his white shirt, blue cotton slacks and black leather boots dirty, he sat perched on the countertop in the kitchen, swinging his legs, watching with interest while Sarah did "girl stuff" to Caitlin's hair.

Sarah glanced over her shoulder and smiled fondly at J.J. "Yes," she said emphatically. "I liked her a lot. She was tough, but she was fair."

"Did you get sent to the principal's office? What did you do? Were you punished?" Caitlin asked, her voice muffled but alive with curiosity. Her head was tipped forward, her chin tucked against her chest while Sarah tied the end of her braid with a narrow red satin ribbon that matched the trim on her white cotton sundress.

Sarah chuckled. "No...nothing...and no. Mrs. Fitch was the principal, but she also taught honors English and I took her class when I was a high school senior."

"So she was a teacher, too?" J.J. asked, his brow wrinkling in confusion.

"Yes." Sarah gave the scarlet ribbon a final, testing tug and stepped back. "All done, Caitlin. Go look in the mirror in the living room."

Caitlin whisked out the door. Sarah lifted J.J. down from the counter and stepped over the threshold just in time to see Caitlin turning slowly in front of the long mirror that hung over the old-fashioned oak sideboard.

"Is that really me?"

Caitlin's voice held awed disbelief. Sarah smiled; Caitlin's standard torn jeans and T-shirt had been replaced by a simple white cotton sundress. The sleeveless bodice with its squared neckline left her throat and arms bare; the full skirt was gathered onto a fitted waist and swirled to her knees. The soft white cotton highlighted her suntanned skin, ebony hair and vivid green eyes.

"Yes," Sarah said with a nod of approval. "That's definitely you."

"Hmm." Caitlin recovered quickly and turned away from the mirror with a self-conscious shrug.

"Jeans are a lot more comfortable, but I guess I can stand wearing a dress for one afternoon."

"Good." Sarah gave her own appearance one last check in the mirror and grabbed her purse and keys from the hall table. "Let's go, guys."

"Race you, Caitlin!" J.J.'s boots clattered across the wooden porch floor as he raced to the car. Caitlin forgot her grown-up image and dashed after him.

The gravel parking lot outside the community center was packed with cars and trucks. Sarah wedged her little compact in between two dusty pickups; J.J. was out of his seat belt and waiting impatiently by the car's back bumper before Sarah could collect her purse and the gaily wrapped book of poetry she'd chosen as a gift for Annabel.

"Mommy, hurry up!"

"I'm coming, J.J. Settle down."

"Trey said there's gonna be a cake as big as Texas. I wanna see."

Caitlin rolled her eyes at Sarah with long-suffering patience. "He was kidding, J.J. The cake can't really be as big as Texas."

"Why not?" the little boy demanded, skipping ahead of his mother and cousin as they reached the sidewalk that led to the front doors of the center.

Sarah didn't listen to Caitlin's answer. She'd both anticipated and dreaded this gathering. While she looked forward to seeing old friends, she wasn't eager to face the inevitable questions about J.J.'s father and her own obviously single status. That Josh would most likely be present with his brother and family added to her apprehension. This birthday party would be the first time since she'd returned that they'd both been present at a social function, and Sarah wasn't at all sure how either of them would react, since Josh was unpredictable at best. She never knew if he would treat her with distant, cold courtesy, or if he would be broodingly angry and explosive.

Not that he doesn't have good cause, she acknowledged with an inner sigh.

"Sarah!"

Wes's deep, booming voice interrupted Sarah's gloomy thoughts. Her uncle's broad figure moved out of the group of men standing just to the left of the main entrance, and he strode toward her.

"Hi, Uncle Wes." J.J. caught his great-uncle's hand and Wes bent to sweep him up.

"How ya doin', J.J.?" Wes tweaked J.J.'s nose and earned a throaty chortle from the little boy.

"Fine, Uncle Wes. Have you seen the cake yet?" J.J. demanded.

"The cake? Nope, not yet. Why?"

"J.J. thinks the cake is going to be huge," Sarah said as she reached the two. Beside her, Caitlin shook her head and sighed.

"I told him that Trey was just teasing, but J.J. won't believe me," Caitlin told her great-uncle.

Wes grinned and winked at Caitlin. "We'll just have to go inside and take a look, won't we, honey? Then J.J. can judge for himself."

Wes swung J.J. to the ground and slung an arm over Caitlin's shoulders. "Molly wants the kids to come spend the night with us," he said to Sarah as they walked through the open double doors and into the wide foyer. "Wayne's staying with us so that Jennifer and Lucas can have a free evening. Molly thought J.J. and Caitlin would be great company for him."

Before Sarah could answer, J.J. caught her hand and tugged her to a halt. "Can we, Mommy? Please? I'll be good, I promise."

Sarah hesitated, torn with indecision; J.J. hadn't spent a night away from her since his birth. Caitlin laid a hand on her forearm to claim her attention and Sarah looked down at her, into green eyes that held an awareness and empathy far beyond her twelve years.

"I'll look after him, Aunt Sarah," she promised solemnly. "I know he sometimes gets scared in the night, but you can trust me—I'll stay with him. I won't leave him alone in the dark."

Sarah's throat closed with emotion, making speech impossible. *How many times were you scared in the dark night with no one to stay with you?* Sarah knew with swift, undeniable surety that she would move heaven and earth to keep Caitlin from going back to Los Angeles.

She cleared her throat. "All right, Caitlin," she said, her voice still thick with emotion. "I know you'll take good care of J.J."

"I'm a big boy. I can take care of myself," J.J. announced, clearly disgusted with the inference that he wasn't grown up.

Wes shot an understanding look at Sarah and ruffled J.J.'s hair with one big hand. "Of course you are, cowboy. Now, let's go take a look at that cake."

He started moving again, clearing a path through the crowd that thronged the foyer and crowded the long communal room beyond. Long tables covered with white cloths were arranged at one end, with a shorter table angled to one side. Wes wove his way around laughing, chatting clusters of people, returning greetings with bluff good humor, but not stopping until the four reached the long table gleaming with silverware and crystal.

"Wow!" J.J. breathed in awe as he stared at the six-tiered cake with its white icing and pink frosting roses. "Is that how big Texas is?"

Wes laughed, his eyes twinkling with amusement as his gaze met Sarah's over J.J.'s fair head. "I think maybe Texas might be a tad bit bigger, J.J., but there's no question that this cake is big."

"Can we eat a piece now?"

"No," Sarah said firmly, capturing J.J.'s hand as his forefinger reached for the tempting icing. "Not until the birthday girl blows out the candles." She tightened her grip when he would have moved away, and bent to hand him Annabel's gift. "Would you like to put Mrs. Fitch's present on the table with the other gifts?"

"Sure." J.J. promptly took the package and, holding it carefully, walked beside Sarah to the smaller table. The white cloth was nearly hidden beneath the colorful, ribbon-tied boxes; J.J. considered the available space for a long moment before placing the package on a corner, with deliberate precision. Then he spun away and skipped a few steps toward the cake table before he halted abruptly.

"Hey! There's Wayne."

"J.J., wait..." Before she could stop him, he raced off across the room, dodging around groups of adults. The clusters of people shifted, opening a path, and Sarah saw J.J. reach Wayne. Jennifer bent to speak to him, her glorious mane of red-gold hair falling forward over her shoulders, and J.J. twisted around, pointing at Sarah. Jennifer looked up, saw Sarah and Caitlin, and straightened. Smiling warmly, she turned to the tall, dark man at her side and spoke animatedly. He turned his head, and Sarah recoiled from the brief flash of black anger in his turquoise eyes before he shuttered the emotion.

If Sarah hadn't recognized Lucas Hightower from her years in Butte Creek, she would have known who he was from the way Jennifer looked at him. Lucas's hard mouth lifted in a half smile, but the fiercely tender affection in his expression and the possessive hand he rested at the small of his wife's back left no doubt that this woman belonged to him.

Sarah's heart ached. She vividly remembered that same expression on Josh's face years before; that she would surely never see him look at her that way again was a pain too deep for tears.

As if her thoughts had called him, Josh walked up to Lucas. His back to her, he was dressed in Western-cut gray slacks and black dress boots, his shoulders broad beneath the fine weave of a white shirt. The long sleeves were folded back over his forearms, the gold band of a watch gleaming against deeply tanned skin. He glanced over his shoulder, snaring her gaze for a taut moment before he turned back, said something to Lucas and bent to speak to J.J.

J.J. nodded eagerly and held out his arms; Josh swung him up and onto his shoulders. Lucas did the same with Wayne and the two big men, Jennifer between them, started toward her.

"Hi, Mommy. Look how high I am!"

J.J.'s crow of delight demanded her attention. Sarah couldn't help but smile back at his ear-to-ear grin.

"Me, too, Sarah," Wayne said firmly. "I'm tall, too."

"You certainly are," Sarah assured him. Her

gaze slipped from Wayne's face to his father's and her smile disappeared. Lucas's austere features held none of the open, friendly acceptance that shone from Wayne's.

"You know my husband, Lucas, don't you, Sarah?" Jennifer asked, breaking the small silence.

"Yes," Sarah said quietly. "Hello, Lucas."

"Sarah." Lucas nodded briefly, but his hands didn't move from their loose grip on Wayne's ankles.

Sarah didn't offer her hand. Although Lucas was polite, his distant reserve wasn't encouraging.

"Have you had a chance to visit with Annabel yet?"

Josh's deep voice drew Sarah's gaze from Lucas. His turquoise eyes, so like his brother's, held heat that had nothing to do with anger.

"No, we haven't." Sarah glanced at Jennifer. "Have you?"

"Lucas and I have," Jennifer replied. "But Josh hasn't. Why don't you three go say hello and wish her a happy birthday, and then meet us over there." She pointed down the long length of the room where chairs arranged around tables covered with white cloths were gradually beginning to fill with people. "We'll claim a table before all the seats are gone."

"All right." Much as she liked Jennifer, Sarah didn't plan to share the evening with Josh and Lucas. However, she couldn't see a graceful way to decline, nor could she think of a polite way to reject the obvious pairing Jennifer made of her and Josh.

"Ready?" Josh claimed her attention once again. "Annabel is holding court in the corner farthest from the bandstand."

Sarah half turned to follow his gaze, scanning the crowd to find the high school principal seated in a corner, surrounded by well-wishers. Josh's hand brushed against her waist to move her gently ahead of him and she jerked involuntarily, stepping hurriedly away from his touch.

"I don't see Caitlin, do you?" she asked, refusing to meet his eyes and the questioning frown that darkened his features. "I wanted to introduce her to Mrs. Fitch."

"She's with Aunt Molly," J.J. said. "Over by the door."

"So she is." Sarah glanced up at Josh. "I'll collect her and meet you two in the corner."

"All right." Josh stood for a moment, watching Sarah's slim back as she wound her way through the throng toward Molly and Caitlin. Sarah was a puzzle that baffled him. The more he observed her, the more frustrated and confused he became.

J.J.'s small hand gently patted his cheek, demanding his attention.

"Josh? Hey, Josh, are we gonna go see Mrs. Fitch?"

"Sure, cowboy." Diverted, Josh tugged on a

miniature boot and was rewarded by a giggle from J.J. "Don't bump your head on the rafters."

"I won't, but I'm high enough to touch the ceiling almost!"

The two threaded their way down the length of the room and stood on the edges of the crowd surrounding Annabel, patiently waiting their turn.

Sarah and Caitlin joined them just as they reached Mrs. Fitch.

"Well, hello, Josh. And who is this young man?"

"I'm J.J. and I'm four," the little boy announced importantly from his lofty perch atop Josh's broad shoulders.

Mrs. Fitch's eyes twinkled and she pushed her glasses higher on her nose, tipping her head back to look up at him. "Hello, J.J. I'm Annabel and I'm sixty."

"Wow." J.J.'s eyes rounded. "That's really old, huh?"

Mrs. Fitch laughed while Sarah groaned and shook her head.

"J.J., it's not polite to comment on a lady's age." Josh winked at Mrs. Fitch and grinned.

"Nonsense," Annabel declared with amusement. "I've earned every one of these gray hairs and J.J.'s right, sixty is really old. But there are some benefits to being really old," she said confidingly. "The birthday parties get bigger and better the older you get."

"Yeah," J.J. replied promptly. "You've got a really big cake, but Trey said it was as big as Texas and Caitlin said it wasn't either. Do you know how big Texas is?"

"Very big," the principal responded solemnly. "I don't think the cake is quite as big as Texas—but it's definitely big."

"I think so, too." J.J. smiled benevolently at her, clearly pleased that she wisely agreed with him.

"Then we agree." Mrs. Fitch nodded firmly before turning to hold out her hands. "Sarah, it's so good to see you."

Sarah caught Annabel's fingers with hers. The older woman's hands were crippled with arthritis, but her grip was strong and warm. Sarah bent forward and brushed a kiss against her cheek.

"It's wonderful to see you, too, Mrs. Fitch. Happy birthday."

"Thank you. And who is this young lady?"

Sarah slipped an arm around Caitlin's shoulders and drew her forward. "This is my niece, Caitlin, Margaret's daughter. She lives with her mother in Los Angeles but is spending the summer with us."

"Ahh," Mrs. Fitch's blue eyes were shrewd but kind as they inspected the twelve-year-old's impassive expression. "You look like your mother, child." She reached out and gently took Caitlin's hand in both of hers. "I'm delighted that you're here to help your aunt Sarah while your grandmother is ill.'' She glanced at Sarah. "How is Patricia, Sarah?''

Josh only half heard the conversation as Sarah and Annabel exchanged information and chatted about family and mutual acquaintances. J.J.'s solid little body sitting on his shoulders and Caitlin and Sarah by his side created a picture of a family. He wished he had the right to claim them as his. The need to do so was a bittersweet, piercing pain.

He moved restlessly, bumping the man behind him.

"Sorry,'' he muttered over his shoulder before turning to Sarah. "Maybe we should move on and give the rest of these folks a chance to say hello.''

"Oh, certainly.'' Sarah glanced at the lengthening line behind Josh. "Perhaps we'll have a chance to talk more later.''

"Absolutely,'' Annabel said promptly. "And if not, then call me next week and we'll have lunch.''

"It's a date,'' Sarah agreed.

Josh bent and brushed a kiss against Mrs. Fitch's cheek, eliciting a shriek of delighted terror from J.J.

"Happy birthday. Save a dance for me,'' Josh told her.

"I'll do that.''

Behind them, the band began to play, the music filling the big hall. Sarah led the way down the length of the room, but veered to the left halfway to the table where Jennifer sat with Lucas.

Josh caught her elbow and she halted instantly,

slipping out from beneath his loose hold immediately.

"What is it?" she asked, her voice lifting to be heard above the noise of the crowd and the music.

"You're going the wrong way." He gestured toward Lucas. "Our table's down this way."

"I promised Molly and Wes that we'd join them, and they're over in that corner."

Sarah gestured and Josh's gaze followed, easily finding Wes's broad bulk. Before he could object, Sarah reached up and plucked J.J. from his grasp.

"I'm sure we'll see you later, Josh. Thank you for looking out for J.J."

Josh stood still, the crowd ebbing and flowing around him, and once more watched Sarah's slender back as she walked away from him.

I'm getting damn tired of seeing her walk away, he thought grimly. He spun on his heel and stalked down the room to join Lucas and Jennifer.

He sat with the rest of the Hightower clan, including Murphy—his leg encased in a walking cast—and Trey, while speeches were given, food was served from a buffet table groaning under laden platters and bowls, and presents were opened by Annabel. Never did he lose track of Sarah, though. The internal radar that responded only to her kept him always aware of her movements as she supervised J.J. and Caitlin through the buffet line, wiped cake frosting from J.J.'s chin and kept an eye on a group of preteen boys who were ogling Caitlin.

The evening waned, the sun setting and dusk falling outside. Plates were emptied, coffee cups drained, and couples began to drift onto the impromptu dance floor at the end of the hall nearest to the bandstand.

Wes lifted a sleepy J.J. to his shoulder and dropped an arm around Caitlin's shoulders before heading toward the door. Josh's eyes narrowed, his gaze tracking Sarah as she and Molly wound their way to Annabel's side. Clearly, the two women were saying good-night.

"To hell with it," Josh muttered, and pushed away from the table. He was going to claim a dance with Sarah. Holding her would be sweet torture, but the need was stronger than the pain that would surely follow.

Sarah was several steps behind her aunt Molly when a man caught her forearm, stopping her. Her heart raced with swift fear and she spun around, nearly tumbling against Josh's chest.

"Oh!" She stepped quickly backward, slipping her arm from beneath his grip. Her palm pressed over her thundering heart, she managed a weak smile. "You startled me."

"Sorry, I didn't mean to." He stared down at her. "Dance with me."

Her pale brows winged upward in surprise.

"Just once...for old times' sake," he said abruptly, certain that she was going to refuse.

Her gaze darkened, sorrow and pain clearly visible before she shook her head and stepped back. "I'm sorry, Josh. I can't. I never dance anymore."

She turned swiftly and left him.

Once again Josh found himself staring at her retreating figure.

Fury roared through him, fueled by hurt and frustration.

I'll be damned if I'll let her walk away from me again!

He strode after her, moving across the threshold of the anteroom just as she stepped outside the building. Quickening his steps, with his long strides he overtook her just beyond the entrance.

"Wait a minute," he growled.

Startled, Sarah caught a glimpse of his set, furious expression before his fingers locked around her upper arm and he drew her swiftly around the corner of the building. Away from the entrance lights, this side of the community hall was shadowed and dark.

"I'm getting tired of watching your cute backside moving away from me," he snapped. He pushed her up against the wall and lowered his head, unerringly finding her mouth with his.

Sarah was so stunned by the swift, unexpected events that she didn't react, her fear of men held at bay by the fact that this was Josh.

Chapter Eight

The anger that drove Josh to claim Sarah in the most primitive way known to males was quickly swamped by need. Emotionally and physically starved for the scent, feel and warm reality of her, Josh cradled her head in his palms, threading his fingers through her hair to hold her still while his mouth made sweet, heart-stopping love to hers.

So stunned was Sarah that she didn't close her eyes; she watched the anger driven from his features and replaced by ardent, tortured tenderness. Fierce absorption drew his brows together in a frown of concentration, his thick lashes lying in feathery black crescents against sun-dark skin. Faint white lines fanned out at the corners of his eyes, mute testimony to long hours spent beneath the prairie's hot summer sun.

This was Josh—and she loved him. For one long, hope-filled moment, Sarah dared to believe that this time might be different.

But then Josh moved closer, pinning her between the wall and the hard, implacable strength of his body. Her eyes slammed shut and she fought the suffocating panic that threatened her. Josh shifted, aligning his body with hers, and the hard proof of arousal pressed against her midsection sent her over the edge. She was no longer able to hold terror at bay, and her fear demanded she focus on survival. She struggled, shoving frantically against his chest.

Sarah went so abruptly from warm acceptance to violent rejection that Josh didn't have time to react. Once again he found himself watching her run away—this time across the parking lot to her car. Too dazed to chase her, Josh leaned against the wall and stared after her until her car's taillights disappeared from view.

The longer he leaned against the wall, the more his head cleared. And the more his certainty grew that she had just given him a missing piece to the puzzle that was Sarah.

"You didn't just run from the heat between us, Sarah," he mused, narrowed eyes staring unseeingly down the now-dark road. The glimpse he'd caught of her face before she ran was etched with sharp clarity in his mind. "You were terrified of something. What was it?"

He forced himself to go over all the times he'd seen Sarah since she'd returned. Putting aside his own bias, he struggled to remain objective and analytical.

"She never touches anyone male, except J.J.— not even her uncle Wes." The memory of her slipping away from her uncle on the porch at the Rocking D was clear, followed swiftly by the knowledge that she'd avoided any contact with him with equal determination. The stark terror on her face when the doctor had touched her shoulder at the hospital was the same deep level of panic he'd seen only moments before when she'd run away from him.

The picture that was forming wasn't pretty, but Josh couldn't avoid the ugly conclusion that he reached.

"Son of a bitch," he breathed, his chest lifting painfully as he dragged air into tortured lungs. "Somebody hurt her—really hurt her. She's afraid of men."

But who? Her father had doted on her, as had Josh. It had to have been someone in her life after she'd left Butte Creek five years ago. And the most likely candidate was J.J.'s other possible father.

I'm tired of guessing, he thought grimly. *Only Sarah knows what happened—and tonight she's going to give me answers.*

He pushed away from the wall and strode across the gravel lot to his truck.

Sarah hadn't expected Josh to follow her. Angry with herself for the foolish tears that wouldn't obey her command to cease, she stomped up the stairs, stripped off her clothes and climbed into the shower. The hot water sluiced away the tears and all but traces of self-disgust, and she dried her hair with brisk strokes before pulling on her favorite, comfortable blue terry-cloth robe.

Downstairs in the kitchen, she brewed coffee and rummaged in the freezer for a chocolate bar. She was determined not to give in to misery over her failure to control the mindless terror that had destroyed her pleasure and overwhelmed her in Josh's arms.

She was muttering and ripping the wrapping off a candy bar when someone knocked at the back door.

Startled, she stopped tearing paper and stared at the darkened porch off the kitchen.

"Who in the world...?"

Knuckles rapped impatiently once again. Sarah hurried to the window, pulled back the curtain and leaned over the sink to peer out at the front of the house. Parked outside her gate was Josh's truck.

"Oh, no," she whispered. Her nerveless fingers lost their grip, the forgotten curtain dropping back into place.

Josh knocked again. "Sarah? Sarah! I know you're in there. Open the door."

Reluctantly Sarah crossed the kitchen and the small utility porch, hesitating before she drew a deep breath and pulled the door open.

The light from the kitchen shafted across the porch and found Josh's broad-shouldered figure standing on the back step. Grim-faced, he stared at her for a long moment before she gave way, stepping aside to let him into the house.

"I don't suppose this is a social call?" Resignation colored her voice.

"No," he said briefly. This time it was Josh who stepped aside, waiting silently for her to move past him and into the kitchen.

"I'm having coffee," she said, her back to him as she stood at the counter. She glanced over her shoulder. "Would you like some?"

"Sure." Josh's gaze moved assessingly over her features. She wasn't wearing makeup, and her eyes were dark pools of shadowed, stormy blue in her pale face. Her mouth was bare of lipstick, her lips and the arch of her cheekbones soft pink against barely tanned skin. There was a fragile vulnerability about her, oddly reinforced by the determination evident in the tilt of her chin and the proud set of her shoulders. He suspected that the soft blue robe was all she wore; he shoved the instant mental picture of Sarah's naked body out of his mind and grimly ignored the leap of his pulse. "What I really want are some straight answers."

Sarah expelled her held breath in a deep sigh. "I was afraid of that," she said, not even bothering to pretend she didn't understand what he meant. She reached for a mug from the cupboard and poured coffee before looking up at him again. "Would it make any difference if I told you that you won't want to hear the answers—that you'll wish you'd never asked?"

"No." He bit out the word. "And I can't say I appreciate your treating me as if I were J.J.'s age. Whatever you have to tell me, it can't be worse than not knowing."

The look Sarah gave him was laden with weary resignation. She handed him the mug and cradled her own cup between her palms.

"Oh, yes, it can, Josh. I'd hoped that we would never have to have this conversation, but it seems I asked for too much."

"Maybe so." Too angry and frustrated to be put off yet again, Josh set the hot mug down on the tabletop and ignored the reluctance that gripped her. "I still want answers. Why did you run away from me tonight? What happened to you in the years you were gone from Butte Creek that makes you run from me and avoid your uncle?"

"I was raped the night I left Butte Creek."

Her blunt words chased the anger from Josh's face and replaced it with stunned shock. Instinctively, he moved toward her, his arms lifting to hold her, but she shifted closer to the counter at her back and he halted immediately, his hands slowly falling to curl into fists at his side. Her fragile shell of calm composure protected a deep well of emotion behind its thin walls. He was afraid of what it might do to her if he shattered that defense.

Shock and compassion were swiftly replaced by a surge of anger. *Why didn't she tell me?*

Of all the possible scenarios that Josh's imagination had considered in the past half hour, none of them had come even close to her response. Shaken by a wave of emotions that ranged from shock to rage and grief that someone had hurt her, his first instinct was to hold her close. He ached to give her comfort, but her flinching away told him clearly that she couldn't accept it.

"Ah, sweetheart." His voice sounded thick and rusty to his own ears, clogged with emotion. "Can you talk about it?"

Sarah nodded jerkily. She'd never wanted to have this conversation, but now that she'd started, she wanted it finished. The fact that Josh hadn't exploded and demanded to know why she'd let the attack happen, nor accused her of lying, nor any of the other all-too-common negative responses was encouraging.

"Let's sit down." Josh pulled out a chair at the table. She seemed calm and composed, but he hadn't missed the tremor that shook her fingers nor the dark, haunted look in her eyes. Unwilling to crowd her, he stepped back, waiting for her to slip into a seat before taking a chair across from her. He waited for her to begin, sipping coffee that he didn't want and didn't really taste, while he forcibly held back the barrage of questions that trembled on his tongue.

"I tried to call you before I left Butte Creek that afternoon," Sarah began. She sat stiffly upright in her chair, forearms resting on the tabletop, her fingers clasped around the comforting warmth of her coffee mug. "Great-Aunt Prudence fell and strained her back and Mother asked me to go to Missoula to stay with her. The hospital wouldn't let her go home alone." Sarah flicked a glance upward at Josh. "She's my favorite relative. I was more than willing to take care of her. But I couldn't get you on the phone. I asked Mother to try to reach you, but knowing Mother, I doubted that she would. I planned to stay overnight in Great Falls and drive on to Missoula the following morning, and I knew I could call you from the hotel, so I wasn't terribly worried about reaching you."

She paused, and silence stretched in the brightly lit room. Only the sound of the clock ticking broke the quiet.

"I never got to call you. I checked in to the motel, and a man grabbed me from behind just as I unlocked my door. He shoved me into the room and attacked me." Her sentences were short and choppy, but her voice was blank, without emotion. "When he left, he put the Do Not Disturb sign on the outside doorknob. The motel cleaning staff didn't find me for two days. They called the ambulance. The hospital called my mother. After I was released from the hospital, Mother rented an apartment for me in Great Falls so that I could stay in therapy. It was three weeks before I realized that I was pregnant."

Josh made an inarticulate noise in his throat and she looked up at him. A muscle ticked in his jaw, and his eyes were alive with tortured emotion.

"Why didn't you call me?"

"I wanted to, at first, but later..." Her voice drifted off, pain and regret throbbing in the husky tones. She forced herself to continue her story. "Anyway, I was pregnant. Mother demanded that I have an abortion."

"Why didn't you?" Josh couldn't hold back the question.

"Because I didn't know if it was our baby." Her gaze met his, unconsciously pleading for his understanding. "I was barely able to function—both emotionally and physically—but I knew I wanted our baby. I couldn't bring myself to destroy a child that we might have created when we'd made love."

The instant, leaping blaze of emotion in his eyes reassured her and she dropped her glance.

"Mother finally conceded that I was too unwell to make the decision, but she insisted that I give the baby up for adoption at birth. I agreed. I felt I would know when the baby was born whether or not you were the father. I was sure that your genes would dominate over mine and your baby would have black hair and turquoise-blue eyes, not my blond hair and light blue eyes." She shrugged slightly. "But the truth was, after I carried J.J. in my body for nine months, I couldn't bear to give him to someone else to love. He was mine, regardless of who his father was. And then he was born. His hair was silver-blond, like mine, and his eyes were emerald green." Sarah looked Josh squarely in the eye. "No one in my family has green eyes— except for Caitlin, and hers are like her father's. The man who raped me had dark blond hair and brown eyes."

Josh didn't flinch. "What happened to the son of a bitch?" He ground out the question. "Was he arrested?"

"Yes." Sarah nodded. "But I never had to testify at a trial. He confessed to a string of robberies and rapes across Colorado and Montana and was returned to Colorado for trial. He was killed in a prison fight a year later."

Josh wasn't sure if he was glad or not. He ached to get his hands on the man; red-hot rage at the man who'd dared to hurt her filled him with blood lust. "I see," he managed to say.

"Mother was furious when I told her I was going to keep J.J.," Sarah continued. "She told me that

I couldn't bring him home to Butte Creek. She said our reputation would be ruined and the disgrace would be unbearable."

Josh leaned forward, his body tense. "You let your mother keep you away all this time?"

"Partly, but it wasn't just my mother, Josh." Sarah's own body tensed, her fingers holding on to her cup with punishing force, as if the action would ground her. "By the time J.J. was born, I'd been in therapy for nine months, learning to deal with the trauma of being attacked. I remained in intensive counseling for three months after his birth, but I couldn't get past my fear of men." She lifted her gaze to his, her expression sad but resigned. "I just couldn't, Josh. I'm still incapable of enduring physical contact with a male. It took months for me to be able to get on an elevator if there was a man inside." She gestured with her hand at the kitchen. "That's why J.J. and I are here instead of Aunt Molly's. Uncle Wes is used to giving me affectionate hugs—but I can't bear to have him put his arms around me. I can't tell him why." A brief, bitter smile twisted her mouth. "He might understand, but the truth is, most people don't want to hear about it. They don't want to know this happened to someone they love."

"Is that why you didn't tell me?" Josh asked tightly.

"Partly," Sarah admitted. "But more because I had nothing to offer you, Josh. I'll never be able to be physically intimate with a man, so marriage is out of the question. I'm incapable of giving any man what he has a right to expect from his wife—an intimate, satisfying male-female relationship.''

"Did he…'' Josh stopped and cleared his throat. "Did he hurt you? Was there physical—''

"No,'' Sarah said hastily. "It's emotional. I can't control my emotional reaction—I know it's not rational. The counselor said it was like being claustrophobic—I just can't seem to get past the terror.''

"And that's why you wrote me that letter?''

"Yes.''

"I thought you'd found someone else.''

"I'm sorry, Josh.'' Her heart hurt at the brief flash of desolation in his blue eyes. "I thought I was doing the right thing,'' she whispered painfully. "There was no future for us, and I wanted you to forget me and go on, to be happy—''

"Happy?'' Josh searched the fragile contours of her face. "Is that what you are? Happy?''

Sarah was silent for a moment, considering. "I don't know that I'm happy, Josh. I've come to accept that my life is limited to my work and J.J.''

Josh struggled with rage at the man who'd hurt her, frustration that she'd waited five years to tell him, pain for the struggle she'd endured, and his own anger and hurt that she hadn't trusted him enough to share that struggle with him.

He sighed heavily and scrubbed his hand over

his face. "Sarah…" he said wearily. "What the hell are we going to do about this?"

"Nothing," she answered softly. He looked up quickly, disbelievingly. "Nothing. There isn't anything we can do without one of us getting hurt even more. A long time ago I accepted that I only have J.J. to love. He's the only male I'll ever be able to hold."

Josh disagreed. He had an instinctive, primal need to deny that her future held only J.J.

"If none of this had happened five years ago," he said, his gaze intent on hers, "did you love me enough to marry me?"

Sarah didn't hesitate. "Yes."

He didn't doubt her. The soft, emotion-filled, single word ripped through his chest and straight into his heart.

"And I loved you." He watched tears spring into her eyes as he said the quiet words, and hope budded slowly, unfurling tiny green shoots in the desert wasteland that for so long had been his heart. He reached for her, his hands closing over hers where they wrapped around her mug. With careful patience his fingers gently pried hers loose and cradled them in his own. "If we'd been married back then, before it happened, what would you have done, Sarah?"

Sarah stared at him. His lashes were lowered, his gaze fastened on the tabletop where her hands lay sheltered in his much bigger, darker ones. Callused palms up, his hands held hers loosely, her palms resting against his while his thumbs moved in gentle, soothing, rhythmic strokes across the backs of her hands.

"What would I have done?" Distracted by the slow, brushing movements of his thumbs over her skin, she waited with sick expectancy for the debilitating panic, revulsion and the brassy taste of fear that always accompanied being touched. It didn't come. Sarah's gaze left the sight of their joined hands and lifted to his. He was watching her intently and she frowned faintly. "About what?"

"About us," he said softly. "If you'd legally been my wife, would you have come home to me? Or would you have written that letter?"

"I..." Sarah faltered. Silence stretched while she considered. "I wouldn't have written you a letter," she said finally. "I would have told you in person...and I would have told you the truth."

Josh knew a surge of relief. "And then what?"

"Then..." She paused again, gazing helplessly at him. "I guess what happened next would have been up to you. But, Josh, I still wouldn't have been able to let you touch me."

Josh glanced significantly down at their hands, palm to palm, atop the table.

"I'm touching you now."

"I know," Sarah acceded, her fingertips pressing tentatively, testingly against the hard warmth of his. "And it's more than I've been able to deal with from anyone else—even Uncle Wes. But there's a big difference between holding hands and making love."

"True." Josh nodded. Silence reigned in the kitchen while he considered what she'd told him. "You said you were in therapy for—how long? Nine months?"

"Closer to twelve."

"Were you alone? Or were there other women there?"

"Both. I had individual counseling and then, later, group meetings."

"So you talked to other women who'd been through this?"

"Yes."

"Were any of them married?"

"Yes, quite a few of them were."

"Did they all have the same feelings you have about being touched?"

Sarah nodded slowly. "All of us had difficulties of one sort or another."

"How did the married ones deal with their husbands?"

"You mean, how did they deal with making love?"

"Yeah." Josh's thumbs continued their slow, calming strokes across her hands.

Sarah shrugged. "Some of the men couldn't deal with it. They treated their wives as if they'd been unfaithful. Several of the women in my group were divorced by their husbands within a year or two."

Disgusted, Josh swore under his breath. "What about the others?"

"They struggled," Sarah said simply. "But for most of them, it got better with time."

"So some women do get past this," he said thoughtfully. "Tell me what you feel when you're touched, Sarah. I want to understand."

"Afraid," she whispered. "And threatened—terrified." Her vision lost focus, her gaze turned inward. "And that's just when a man moves within a few feet. I've learned to control the fear—until I'm touched. Then I get cold, sick—all I can see is his face, the noises he made, the pain..." She broke off, visibly collecting herself. "I'm sorry, Josh. I hate that I have no control over my reactions, and I hate talking about this."

Josh fought down the need to grab her and hold her close, forcing himself to speak deliberately and calmly. "Then don't. Instead, let's talk about the married women you knew who got better with time. How did they get well?"

Sarah thought about the women who, supported by loving husbands, had fought their way through the nightmare and survived with their marriages intact.

"They had husbands with infinite patience," she said. His thumbs paused, his fingers tightening against hers. "But none of them were as paranoid about being touched as I was, Josh—as I still am," she added.

"Maybe," he responded quietly. "But you never tried, Sarah. You never let me try."

"I know, but..." *Infinite patience.* Memories of making love with Josh the first time flashed through her mind. He'd had infinite patience with her innocence, even though he'd been shaking with need, sweat pouring from his big body as he held himself in check to assure her pleasure.

Josh watched doubt chase rejection from her expressive features, to be replaced by a tiny flash of hope. That small spark gave him the courage to go on.

"I loved you more than life five years ago, Sarah," he said quietly. "When you left, you took my heart with you. I never got it back. I've been walking around breathing, but I'm dead inside." Tears welled in her eyes, trembling on her lower lashes before spilling over to slide slowly down her cheeks. Josh cupped her chin in one big hand and smoothed a salty drop from the corner of her mouth with the pad of his thumb. "I still love you—I always will. You're mine—you've been mine since the first time we made love. In my heart we're as married as a man and woman can get, even if we didn't have the preacher say the words."

"Josh..." Sarah breathed, tears painfully clogging her throat, stopping her words. His gaze held her, his turquoise eyes dark, intense with emotion.

"Shh," he said softly. "I want my heart back. I want you, Sarah. Well or not, I don't care. I want you to let us try to heal each other. Give us a chance."

She teetered on the edge of indecision, her face giving away the hope that warred with the fear within her. Josh managed a small smile and gently tucked a pale strand of hair behind her ear. He purposely let his fingers linger in the blond silk; though she stiffened with apprehension, she didn't flinch and move away. By the time his fingers brushed the soft skin of her cheek, Sarah was visibly trembling. Still, Josh was encouraged by the yearning that lay beneath the fear in her eyes and the electricity that arced between them when his fingertips stroked gently against the smooth satin skin. He'd often dealt with damaged, abused horses during his many years spent training; he was banking heavily that the same methods of patience and love that had worked for him in the past would work again. Never had he gambled so much, and he refused to contemplate losing.

"Come on," he coaxed gently. "All you have to do is promise to cooperate and trust me not to hurt you. I promise I'll let you make all the moves, and I'll be patient for as long as it takes."

Tempted but unconvinced, Sarah managed a wobbly smile of her own. "What if it takes years?"

Josh shrugged. "It might—or it might not. You've already spent a year in therapy and four more years coming to terms with what happened to you. But even if it takes days, weeks, months or years, we'll be together while we're getting there.''

Sarah's face sobered. ''I don't want you to waste your life waiting for something that might never happen.''

''I don't have a life without you, Sarah.'' His voice held deep conviction.

Regret flooded Sarah. She'd thought she'd saved him pain by keeping him from becoming involved in her limited recovery. Instead, the opposite had happened. Much as she dreaded the strong possibility of failure, she owed him the chance he asked.

She drew a deep breath and withdrew her hand from his. ''I don't know that I believe anything we do will cure me, Josh. But you're right. I never gave you—us—the chance to work through the fear together.'' She squared her shoulders, pushed back her chair and stood to look down at him. ''Where do we start?''

Josh smiled at her, relief flooding through him. ''You're a brave woman, sweetheart. Thank you.''

Sarah shook her head at him. ''I think we both must be slightly insane. You realize we could both get hurt by this?''

''Nothing could hurt worse than the last five years without you.'' He shoved back his chair and rose.

''You're right,'' she said softly. Their gazes tangled, the pain of long years without each other lying unspoken between them. "So..." Sarah's voice was husky with emotion. "Where do we start?"

"You decide," he answered.

Sarah stared at him. He was so big—broader than her, taller than her, stronger than her and easily a hundred pounds heavier than her. Still, he waited patiently, his very lack of motion quieting her instinctive uneasiness.

"Do you want to go upstairs?" she asked, testing him.

Josh's muscles tensed, his body responding to her words with a surge of hot arousal. "If that's what you want, honey."

"All right," she said with decision. "We'll go upstairs." She turned on her heel and left the kitchen. And even though Josh allowed several feet of space between them, her spine tingled with awareness, anticipation and dread.

The door to her bedroom stood open and Sarah halted abruptly on the threshold. She'd switched the lamp on earlier, and the small globe cast a circle of golden light over turned-down sheets on the four-poster bed. The rest of the room was in shadows, creating a mysterious, seductive intimacy from the familiar furnishings.

Uneasy, Sarah forced herself to step into the room, watching Josh as he, too, moved over the threshold and then past her. He stopped, slowly surveying the room and its furnishings before his gaze returned to rest on her.

"We won't do anything you don't want, honey," he said softly, assessing the swift throb of her pulse at the base of her throat and her fingers clenched around the sash of her robe. "Do you want to go back downstairs?"

Through sheer will, Sarah managed to force her tense muscles to ease slightly. She shook her head. "No."

"All right." He stood perfectly still, hands thrust into his pockets, and waited. The silence stretched. "What do you want to do first?"

Sarah tugged the fingers of one hand through her hair. "I don't know, Josh. I've never had a man in my bedroom before." Nerves strung tight, she frowned at him. "Can't we just get into bed and get this over with?"

If Josh's emotions hadn't already been walking a tightrope, he would have laughed aloud at the exasperation in her voice and on her face.

"We can get in bed," he agreed solemnly. "But first I have to take off my boots." He crossed the room with slow, steady strides. Bending, he caught the top sheet and light blanket, half tossing, half folding them to the foot of the bed before he sat on the edge of the mattress, his thigh nudging the lace-edged pillow. Expecting any moment for her to tell him to stop, he tugged off his boots and set them aside before he looked back at her. "Do you want me to take off anything else?"

Understanding dawned slowly and Sarah's pulse

quickened. "Do I get to decide everything we do?" she asked carefully, determined to define the limits of her control and understand the rules.

"Yes," he said simply.

"Will you stop if I need you to?"

"Yes." Josh saw interest gain dominance over the grim determination and fear in her eyes.

"Will you hate me if I panic? If I can't...if I fail you?"

"Honey, nothing you do tonight could be a failure. You've already given me more than I ever believed we could have again."

Reassured, Sarah walked on trembling legs across the room and halted, one arm curving around the smooth cherrywood post nearest Josh at the foot of the bed.

"In that case—take your shirt off." He reached for the top snap but she stopped him before he popped it open. "No, wait."

Josh halted immediately.

"I'll take it off."

Josh's pulse leapt and he struggled to ignore a swift flood of heat. He'd been fighting the rush of hot blood through his veins ever since Sarah had agreed to make love. He knew, however, from the emotions that moved across her expressive features that she was still struggling to remain calm and not panic. She was far from aroused. He ordered his rampaging hormones to shut down. *Patience,* he reminded himself.

Bent on taking control, Sarah left the support of the polished wood post and stepped forward. Scrupulously avoiding contact with his knees, she stood in front of Josh and leaned forward to reach him. The mother-of-pearl snaps gave easily under her careful tugs, the white cotton separating to let the shirt fall open over his chest. Her gaze never strayed from the snaps beneath her fingers, but even if memory hadn't provided her with a vivid picture, she would have been aware of the width of his sun-bronzed chest and the triangle of silky black curls that arrowed downward over the washboard muscles of his midriff.

She reached the last snap above his belt and paused, glancing up at him.

Josh saw her falter and he lifted one hand, silently asking her to unsnap his cuff. She complied and he repeated the gesture with his other hand before he tugged the shirt from his slacks, shrugged his arms free and tossed it over his shoulder. His gaze never left hers, and neither of them noticed when the shirt landed in a heap on the floor beyond the bed.

"Now what?" she managed to get out.

Josh watched the tip of her tongue flick out to dampen her lips, and he swallowed a groan.

"Do you think you could kiss me?" Her eyes widened, refusal flaring as her gaze flicked downward to his mouth then back up. "I won't grab you, Sarah." His voice was husky. "I promise."

Sarah glanced at his hands; they rested palms down on his thighs. *This is Josh,* she reminded herself. *He won't hurt me—he promised.*

Her gaze locked with his, she leaned forward and carefully brushed her lips against his before easing away. Barely two inches separated their faces; his chest lifted in a heavy sigh, his breath ghosting over her lips as he exhaled. A slow smile tilted the hard line of his mouth. Between the thick black lashes that framed them, his eyes were hot shards of brilliant turquoise.

"You have the softest, sweetest mouth, Sarah. Kiss me again."

Reassured, Sarah brushed his mouth with hers once more. Then again—until her lips lingered, lured into staying by his. His lashes drifted closed, but Sarah continued to watch him. Memories stirred, roused by the feel of his mouth beneath hers. Her body flushed and warmed, heated by Josh and the long-denied, repressed need for him that rose relentlessly, submerging her fear.

Silence filled the room, broken only by the sound of quickening breaths and incoherent murmurs. Sarah's fingers threaded through Josh's hair, her palms cradling his skull. Long moments passed before she lifted her head, breathless, to look at him. His lashes lifted and she caught her breath at the hot, naked desire that lay in his eyes.

Her fingers tightened and she eased backward. One swift downward glance told her that his body was blatantly aroused; his hands no longer lay palms downward on his thighs. Now they were curled into tight fists.

"Sarah." His voice was a full octave lower, gravelly with need. "I can't stop my body's reaction to you. That's something I've never been able to control. I can't hide how much I want you, but I won't do anything about it, not unless you want me to."

Her gaze rose to meet his, and Josh sucked in a swift breath at the heated longing in her eyes. Her lips were damp, softly swollen from the long contact with his. His body clenched with need and he stared at her mouth, silently willing her to come back to him.

When she slowly lowered her mouth to his, he strained to meet her until her mouth parted and the tip of her tongue glided across his lower lip. He groaned with satisfaction and returned the sleek, hot caress, his mouth luring her closer.

The simmering heat moving through Sarah's veins pulsed hotter, faster, flooding rich, hot desire through her body. Beneath the soft terry cloth of her robe, her breasts ached, and even the soft robe was unbearably abrasive against the sensitive, swollen tips. She murmured in frustration and Josh shifted, making space for her between his thighs. One small step brought her upper torso flush against his bare chest.

Josh groaned and dragged his mouth from hers.

"Untie your robe, Sarah. I want your skin against mine."

Sarah was immersed in seduction, blindsided by her body's amazing and completely unexpected response to making love with Josh. His harsh, guttural words penetrated the sensual haze that surrounded her, and for a moment fear nudged its way into her consciousness, dulling the edges of delight.

She shoved it away. She refused to give way to panic and terror. The soaring pleasure of making love with Josh had been too long absent from her life.

Deliberately, she flattened her hands over the warm, sleek muscles just below his collarbone and stroked the sensitive pads of her fingertips downward until flat male nipples nudged her palms. They peaked under the brush of her fingers and Sarah stared at them, repeating the movement. Josh shuddered, the muscles of his biceps and chest flexing in response each time she touched him. Fascinated, she looked up at him to find his eyes hot, and dull red streaked across his cheekbones.

"Sarah..." he managed to say.

Sarah undid the sash to her robe, and the blue terry cloth fell open down the front from neck to hem. She barely heard Josh's harsh, indrawn breath before her mouth returned to his and she eased her body carefully against him. His skin was hot, burning up where her softer curves fit against the hard symmetry of his. He shifted, dragging his chest against the swollen, aching tips of her breasts, and Sarah gasped, eagerly repeating his movement, shuddering with pleasure.

Three times eight is twenty-four. Four times eight is thirty-two. Five times eight is...uh... Josh fought for control, his fingers clenched into fists so tight that his knuckles were numb. His body was screaming at him to wrap Sarah in his arms, roll her beneath him, and bury himself in her soft, wet heat.

He couldn't. Having Sarah make love to him was heaven. Not being able to hold her was hell. Especially now, when she was rubbing her bare breasts back and forth against his chest until he thought he'd surely lose what little sanity he had left.

The only consolation was that arousal had chased the fear from her blue eyes. She wanted him. Still, he wasn't sure how much longer he could hold on. He teased the tip of her tongue with his, luring her deeper, and let his muscles relax by degrees until he fell back on the bed. Arms wrapped around his neck, her tongue held captive by his, Sarah went with him, sprawling on top of his prone torso.

Startled, Sarah lifted her mouth from his and looked down at him.

"Don't you think it's time I took my slacks off?" he asked softly.

Fear leapt, striking at Sarah. She'd been side-tracked by the pleasure of touching Josh without thinking beyond the magic of kisses and skin against skin. Now she was forced to think about the reason they'd come to her bedroom. She wasn't sure she could carry this experiment through to its final conclusion, but she was committed to trying.

I don't have to like it, she told herself with fatalistic reasoning. *I just have to get through it.*

"Yes," she said aloud. "I suppose it's time you got undressed." Self-conscious, she gathered the lapels of her robe together and slipped off him to lie curled on her side, the blue terry cloth shielding her bare body, while Josh sat on the edge of the bed and stripped off his slacks. He stretched out beside her, and reached above him to curl his fingers around the bottom edge of the headboard. His body nudged against hers, furnace-hot where her bent knees bumped against his hair-roughened thighs. She straightened one leg and trailed her toes down his calf to his foot, watching his eyes close and his muscles flex and tighten in reaction to the caress. She repeated the movement and his eyes flicked open.

"Come back to me," he whispered, his voice husky, tight with need. She hesitated, and his fingers tightened over the wood.

"I'm afraid," she breathed.

"I know you are." Josh ached for the battle she fought between desire and fear. He wanted to tell her that they didn't need to finish this—that she could return to the safe, sterile emotional zone she'd created for herself. But he knew she wasn't really happy alone there, and he wasn't happy without her. If there was to be a future for them, they had to get past this first time together. "Come up here and kiss me again," he coaxed. "I love your mouth, Sarah."

Sarah knew he was purposely luring her back to him. His patience with her fears when his body was obviously demanding more than kisses soothed the rising tide of terror and allowed sanity and determination to gain control of her emotions.

She pushed up on her knees, carefully straddling his midsection before she bent forward to reach his mouth. Once again her robe fell open, baring the front of her from head to toe. Briefly suppressed by fear, the wanting blazed anew, leaping to life with the roar of wildfire at the touch of his mouth beneath hers, and Sarah's knees gave way, her body easing down atop his. She squirmed instinctively, seeking and settling the cove of her hips over his. Josh responded with a slow, upward thrust, and Sarah's fingers clutched at his shoulders, her fingernails scoring half-moons against his skin.

Josh clenched the headboard until his fingers went numb.

"Sarah," he murmured against her mouth. Her eyes were dark, dazed when they met his. He squeezed his fingers tighter and fought down the unbearable urge to take her. "Take me. Now." He could barely get the words out.

She stared at him for a taut, tension-filled moment before she reached between them and freed him from the soft cotton briefs. He surged against the soft skin of her belly and she stiffened, glancing down the length of their bodies where she lay against him.

"Sarah, look at me."

She obeyed and found him staring at her, his gaze intense, compelling.

"Don't look away. Don't close your eyes," he demanded hoarsely. "I want you to know who's here with you."

She nodded, unable to speak.

His body tightened in reaction, and his arousal brushed against her hand. He was hot silk over steel when her fingers closed around him.

His breath hissed in, his irises turning molten turquoise. "Sarah, please..."

Sarah felt a surge of power that was seductive, arousing. Josh could have taken what he needed by the sheer force of his physical strength. Instead, he lay beneath her, allowing her the choice of ending his torment or denying him satisfaction.

Control was freeing and infinitely satisfying, empowering and exhilarating. The rush of power stoked sexual need, turning the flames that licked at her body into a firestorm. Without taking her gaze from his, she slowly took him into her body, easing downward until he was seated deep inside her.

Josh struggled for control and lost. Dimly, he remembered not to let go of the headboard, but his body took over, thrusting up into the tight, wet heat of hers until sweet release claimed him. It wasn't until he collapsed against the tangled sheet, dragging air into starving lungs, that he realized he couldn't remember what had happened to Sarah.

Oh, no. Foreboding mixed with anxiety as he tried desperately to remember. The soft weight of her body sprawled atop his eased his fear, and his tense muscles relaxed slightly.

"Sarah?" he whispered softly into the tangled blond silk brushing the underside of his chin.

"Mmmhh?"

The drowsy, sated satisfaction in her low murmur was a relief, and Josh slowly relaxed his grip on the wooden headboard. His joints felt locked in place, and he had to forcibly stretch each finger to make them release.

"Are you all right?" he asked cautiously.

Sarah stirred. Unwilling to move, she merely nodded. The hard body she lay against tensed.

"Are you sure? I didn't hurt you, did I?"

She pushed her hair out of her eyes and lifted her head, resting her forearms on his chest to look down at him. Worry darkened his eyes.

"No, Josh." She smiled as the tension eased from his body and the dark concern faded from his eyes. "You didn't hurt me. In fact, you were wonderful. Thank you."

A slow, heart-stopping smile lifted the hard lines

of his mouth, and Sarah felt her heart beat faster. "You know," she said softly, contemplatively, "I do love you so much it hurts, but that's a different kind of hurt."

Josh's smile faded. "I love you, too, Sarah, so much it hurts." His voice was gravelly and he stopped speaking to clear his throat. "Do you think you could stand it if I put my arms around you, honey?"

Sarah stared at him, gauging the intensity of love and need in his dark turquoise stare. Lying nearly naked against him, she gave him something more important than her body. She gave him trust.

"Yes."

Slowly Josh closed his arms around her, the weight of his hands and arms enfolding her. When she tensed but didn't push him away, he carefully cupped the back of her head in one big palm and gently tucked her head beneath his chin.

"Damn," he said unevenly. "This is better than sex."

Startled, Sarah laughed, her breath feathering over his skin. Still buried deep inside her, his body stirred and flexed, reacting to the soft touch. She smiled against his throat.

"Well," he said wryly, feeling her amusement, "almost as good."

For long moments they lay contentedly, savoring the bone-deep pleasure of holding each other, treasuring the freedom to trace sensitive, curious fingertips over soft skin and sleek, hard muscle.

The thick terry-cloth robe still covered Sarah's arms, shoulders and back. Josh plucked at the offending folds. "Do you think we could get rid of this?" he asked. "It's in the way and besides, I'm the only one naked here."

"Hmm." Sarah reluctantly lifted her fingers from testing the smooth skin over his biceps and shrugged out of the robe. "If I remember correctly, you haven't an ounce of modesty in your entire body. Being naked doesn't bother you at all."

Josh chuckled and tossed the robe onto the floor. "Life doesn't get any better than being naked with you, but it's better when you're naked, too."

Sarah turned her mouth against his throat, the tip of her tongue flicking out to experiment with the taste of faintly salty skin. Josh's muscles tensed beneath her and, deep inside her, his body stretched, seeking and responding to the heat and dampness that gloved him. Her body tightened in instinctive response.

"Sarah?" His voice had gone husky again, faintly slurred. "Do that to me again. Five years is a long, long time."

Startled, Sarah lifted her head and searched his face questioningly.

"Five years," he repeated in answer to her unasked question. "You're not the only one who couldn't stand being touched."

Chapter Nine

"Oh, Josh. I don't know what to say."

"You don't have to say anything." His hands stroked down the satin-smooth skin of her back and closed over the rounded curve of her bottom to press her closer. "Just touch me. I love your hands on me." She responded by tracing the line of his jaw and cheek with her fingers and pressing her lips against the base of his neck. Josh shuddered when she once again tested his pulse with her tongue. "And your mouth," he growled before he bent his head and claimed her lips with his.

It was a long time later before Sarah spoke again. It was 3:00 a.m. and they sat side by side, reclining against pillows propped against the headboard, eating from a tray loaded with what looked like half the contents of her refrigerator.

She munched on a chocolate cookie and watched Josh demolish a chicken drumstick.

"Josh," she began. He glanced up quickly, his slow grin quickly fading when she didn't smile back. "There's something we need to talk about."

"Really?" He wiped his hands and lips on a napkin and gave her his full attention. "What's that?"

"Sex."

"Sex?" He flicked a swift glance over the tangled sheets and the clothing strewn across the bedroom floor. "Didn't we just do that?"

Sarah felt heat move up her cheeks and frowned at him. He smiled innocently back at her, his thick lashes half-lowered over hot blue eyes. "We made love—"

"Yes, we did," he interrupted. "Several times, as a matter of fact."

"Precisely. Each time with me on top."

"Yeah. So?"

"So, I know you like...I remember that you..." The heat in his stare grew and Sarah stopped speaking, her own temperature skyrocketing. "Five years ago we didn't make love the same way every time," she finally finished.

"If you're worried about me getting bored with you on top, Sarah," he began softly, "don't." He laid the palm of one warm, big hand high on her bare thigh. "I'll take you any way I can get you—for now. I won't deny that I've thought about making love with you in the barn, in the bathroom, with you on top, with me on top, standing against the wall in the shower and with you sitting on the kitchen countertop." Josh ignored her startled intake of breath. "We'll get there. In the meantime..." He took the last bite of cookie from her unresisting fingers and dropped it on the tray before he shifted the tray to the floor. Dishes rattled, but he ignored them. "Do that to me again."

He tugged Sarah forward and across his lap.

Josh didn't sleep at all. Sarah dozed, lying sprawled on top of him, but Josh couldn't close his eyes. The wonder of having her in his arms was too profound to allow him to sleep. In the hours before dawn while Sarah slept, Josh faced a truth he could no longer deny. Impossible though it seemed, he loved her more than he had five years before. Bonded as they were by the love they'd shared when they were younger, it seemed that the time they'd spent apart had only deepened and intensified his need for her.

Whatever it takes to keep her here in Butte Creek and in my life, I'll do, he vowed as the sky lightened outside and the first rays of morning sunlight slanted their way through the bedroom and across the foot of the bed.

Sarah stirred, her lashes lifting lazily.

"Josh?"

"Yeah, honey?" His arms tightened and he brushed a kiss against the crown of her head. Soft strands of silky blond hair, subtly scented with roses, brushed his lips and nose. Josh felt drunk on the smell and feel of perfumed hair, satiny skin and warm curves that were uniquely Sarah.

"What time is it?"

Josh turned his head to read the dial of the alarm clock sitting on the bedside table. "Just after five o'clock."

"Mmmh." She snuggled against him and closed her eyes. "Molly isn't bringing J.J. and Caitlin home until eight. We have a whole three hours left to sleep."

Josh felt her body relax and knew that she slept, no doubt exhausted from the hours he'd kept her awake last night. Still, he couldn't fall asleep, and at six-thirty he reluctantly eased out of bed, tucked the sheet over her bare shoulders and silently collected his clothes before padding down the hall to the bathroom.

"Sarah. Sarah, honey. It's time to wake up."

Sarah muttered in protest and turned her face into her pillow, shifting away from the hand that gently shook her shoulder. Seconds later, fingertips brushed her hair from her face and warm lips skimmed damp, teasing kisses over her cheek and ear.

Josh watched Sarah's lips slowly curve into a smile while her eyes remained closed.

"Come on, sunshine," he murmured against the corner of her mouth. "If you don't get out of bed and into the shower, J.J. is going to be in here jumping up and down on top of you."

Sarah's lashes lifted and she looked up at him. He leaned over the bed, his hands braced flat against the mattress on either side of her. She smothered a yawn and stretched lazily. "What time is it?"

"Seven o'clock."

She groaned and lifted a hand to push the hair out of her eyes, heavy lidded and languid. "It can't be. Didn't you just tell me that it was five o'clock?"

"Yup—two hours ago," he said dryly.

"Oh." Her lashes lifted a little higher and she stared at him, frowning slightly. "You're dressed."

"Yeah." Josh watched drowsiness give way to wakefulness and knew the exact moment when uneasy insecurity claimed her. He reached out and stroked a forefinger between her brows, smoothing out the tiny frown lines. "Stop worrying, Sarah. Everything's going to be fine. Go take your shower and then come downstairs. I'll make coffee and we'll talk.''

"All right."

Josh dropped a kiss against her cheek and stood.

Still not completely awake, Sarah caught the edge of the sheet and swung her legs over the edge of the bed before she remembered that she didn't have a stitch of clothes on. She clutched the sheet against her chest, her gaze racing to his, and felt her cheeks heat at the amusement that mixed with masculine appreciation in his eyes.

"Would you hand me my robe, please?" she said with as much dignity as she could muster.

"Sure, honey, where is it?"

"On the back of the door—no, wait." Sarah belatedly recalled Josh stripping her out of the blue terry cloth last night. She searched the room and found the robe lying in a heap in a corner by the bureau. "Over there."

Josh collected the robe and held it out for her to slip into, but she caught a handful of material and tugged it out of his hands. "Sarah," he said, "don't tell me you need to hide behind a sheet and that robe this morning. There isn't an inch of you that I didn't see last night. It's too late to hide from me."

Impatient though he sounded, Sarah didn't miss the worry scarcely hidden beneath his scowl. "All right, fine," she snapped at him, and tossed back the sheet, standing in one smooth movement before shoving her arms into the robe. "Go ahead, have a good look."

She didn't pull the robe closed, and Josh's gaze stroked slowly down, over the smooth curves of rose-tipped breasts, the inward sweep of waist and the shadowy indentation of her navel to the gentle outward swell of her hips and the corn-silk curls at the juncture of her thighs. She was petite, tiny compared to his own height and bulk, and he'd always been amazed at how long her legs were considering her height. He let his gaze linger over her body on his way back up to her face, and by the time he reached her stormy blue eyes, he was painfully hard.

"Damn, woman," he breathed. "Are you trying to kill me? We haven't got time to make love again before the kids get home."

Sarah had meant to assert herself and erase her embarrassment over the fact that she'd instinctively reached to cover herself. Instead, she felt her bones melting at the hot, urgent need she read on Josh's face as he looked at her.

Josh reached out and smoothed his palm slowly over the curve of her breast before he drew a deep breath. With trembling fingers he pulled the edges of her robe together and tied the sash.

"Go get in the shower," he said, his voice unsteady, "before I lose what little control I have left."

He turned on his heel and left the room, leaving Sarah standing silently beside the bed. It wasn't until the sound of his boots on the stair treads ceased and the house was silent that she drew a deep, shaky breath.

"Modesty is not a concept that man understands," she grumbled to herself as she left the bedroom for the shower. But she knew it wasn't lack of modesty that drove him; Josh was refusing to let her put any space between them. She also knew that distancing herself from people had become a defense mechanism she used with everyone. He was right to be wary of its use against him.

The smell of coffee filled the kitchen when Sarah entered the room twenty minutes later. Josh was leaning against the counter, sipping from a steaming mug; his gaze flicked over her from head to toe and back, and his hard mouth lifted in a lazy, appreciative smile, his eyes warm.

"I liked you better naked, but you look like sunshine in that dress."

Sarah glanced down at the yellow sundress she wore and smoothed a hand over her midriff. "Thank you. It's one of my favorites." She crossed the room to the counter and took a mug from the cupboard.

"You were wearing that dress the first time I saw you."

She paused in the midst of pouring coffee and glanced sideways at him. "I was? No, I couldn't have been. I only bought this dress last year."

"I meant the first time I saw you this summer. You crossed the street in front of my truck. It must have been the first day you were back in Butte Creek, because you were wearing it when you came to the ranch house later that afternoon."

"Oh." Sarah finished pouring her coffee and sipped it slowly, turning to lean against the counter. A bare twelve inches of space separated her skirt from his faded jeans. "You remember what I was wearing?"

"I remember everything about you."

"You weren't very happy to see me," Sarah chided him. "You told me to get off the Rocking D and stay off."

Josh shrugged and twisted to set his cup on the countertop behind him. "That was because I didn't want to admit I couldn't deal with having you living and sleeping within walking distance. Before I knew why you left." He gently took the mug from her hands and put it next to his before he cupped her shoulders and moved her in front of him. He tugged carefully and she allowed him to pull her forward until she rested against him, her forearms against his chest, his arms loosely circling her waist, hands linked at the small of her back to keep her close. "Before I met J.J."

Sarah stiffened, her eyes going dark with uncertainty. Josh waited patiently.

"Josh, about J.J...."

She halted, her small white teeth worrying her lower lip. Silence stretched.

"I'd still like to have our blood tested," Josh said quietly. He didn't add that he desperately wanted confirmation that J.J. was really his son. On some level he had the uneasy feeling that it was small-minded of him. Shouldn't he accept J.J. regardless of who his father was? There wasn't any doubt that Sarah and J.J. were a package deal—and Josh really liked the little dynamo. Still, he wanted to know if J.J. was truly his. "You don't have to decide today," he went on, reading the conflicting emotions on Sarah's expressive features. He tucked a strand of blond hair behind her ear and bent to kiss her cheek. "Just think about it, okay?"

Sarah lost herself in the kiss they shared, but she knew that despite the mountains they'd scaled last night, they still faced a seemingly unresolvable issue. Could she bring herself to face conclusive results of blood tests? Could Josh fully accept J.J. without them?

Sarah paused and drew a deep breath, exhaling slowly before pushing open the door to her mother's hospital room. Sunlight streamed into the room, gleaming off the deep red petals of a bowl of roses sitting on the windowsill. Propped against bedpillows, Patricia turned her head and smiled.

"Good morning, Mama," Sarah said cheerily, returning the smile. "I saw Dr. Silas in the hall. He told me that you're ready to leave the hospital."

She bent over the bed to brush a kiss against her mother's cheek and Patricia's smile widened, her blue eyes sparkling with pleased excitement.

"Ye-es." She lifted a hand to indicate the room. "I'm glad. I'm so tired of the smell of antiseptic and these boring white walls."

Sarah dropped her purse on the bedside table and pulled a metal-framed chair closer to the bed.

"Dr. Silas believes that you'd benefit from spending a few more weeks in a rehabilitation program." Patricia's eyes darkened and a frown replaced her smile. "There's an excellent rehab center in Fargo that he recommends very highly."

"I want to go home," Patricia said firmly, her chin set stubbornly. "I'm sick to death of hospitals."

"The rehab center isn't a hospital, Mama," Sarah observed reasonably.

"I don't care," Patricia replied sharply. "It's still not my own bed in my own home."

Sarah sighed. "I know, Mama. I don't blame you for being tired of this. If it were me, I'm sure I would be, too. But wouldn't you rather go to a re-hab center now instead of later? In a few weeks you'll be finished and, except for the possibility of coming back to the hospital for outpatient treatment with a physical therapist, you'll be able to go home for good.''

"I suppose you're right," Patricia said reluc-tantly. "Did Dr. Silas say anything about whether I'll regain full use of my arm?''

"He told me that the prognosis is very good. A lot depends on how hard you work with the thera-pist.''

Patricia's gaze searched Sarah's. At last she seemed satisfied that Sarah was being truthful, and she looked away.

Puzzled, Sarah watched her mother's thin fingers pluck at the bedsheet. "Mama?" Patricia's gaze rose to meet hers. "Is something wrong? Are you worried about therapy?''

"No." Patricia shook her head, her silver-blond hair shifting. She brushed a few vagrant strands from her cheek before dropping her hand to her lap once more. "I have something I need to say to you, Sarah. I know I haven't been an easy patient. Truth to tell, I haven't been an easy parent, either.'' She lifted a hand to stop the denial Sarah was clearly about to offer. "Let me get this said. It's not easy, and I'm not likely to say this more than once in my life, so don't stop me.''

Sarah remained in her seat, listening with growing surprise as her mother continued.

"I could have died from this stroke. I figure God was giving me a warning. And maybe a little more time, if I'm lucky. I know it must seem to you that I always favored Margaret. Well, that wasn't true. It's just that you're very much like your father, and Margaret's very much like me."

Again Sarah nearly interrupted, but Patricia continued doggedly on.

"Margaret was—is—wild, and so was I, when I was young. It wasn't until I met and fell in love with your father that I realized I'd been traveling down a bad road." She squared her thin shoulders and faced Sarah, meeting her gaze without flinching. "There's no disguising the truth. I was a scandal to my poor parents. I turned my back on all that when I married your father and moved to Butte Creek. I vowed that I'd be worthy of him."

Sarah was stunned. Her pious, upright mother had a shady past? "You were, Mama," she said slowly, searching for the right words. "He adored you. You must have known that he did."

"Yes." Tears welled and Patricia dabbed at her lashes with a lace-edged handkerchief. "I know he did. It was such a miracle."

"Did he know?" Sarah asked carefully, wondering just exactly what scandalous things her mother had done.

"Yes, oh yes." Patricia nodded. "And he loved me anyway. That was the amazing thing." She wiped the tears from her cheeks and drew a deep breath. "I'm not blind to the fact that I'm a difficult woman in many ways, Sarah. Like your father, you seem to know that and love me anyway. Not many daughters would have come home to look after a mother who had banished them from their home for five long years. I want you to know that I appreciate everything you've done for me, and that I hope you'll stay in Butte Creek."

"Oh, Mama." Sarah's own chest tightened and her eyes grew damp. She cleared her throat before she could speak. "I'm thinking of staying. J.J. loves it here." She paused a moment, gathering her courage to face the expected outburst from her mother. "Josh and I are trying to work out our differences. There may be a future for us."

The outrage and fury Sarah expected didn't come. Instead, Patricia shook her head, resignation and worry on her face.

"It's difficult for me to object to Joshua Hightower after what I've just confessed to you. But I have to tell you, Sarah, that man is trouble. Unlike your father, he'll never be an easy man to live with."

Relieved, Sarah smiled. "I know, Mama. But you just told me that I'm like Daddy. Maybe the best marriages have one easygoing person paired with one difficult person. It seems to have worked with you and Daddy."

"Hmmph," Patricia snorted, wiping her cheeks with a brisk motion. "I don't know that I like the thought of you comparing me to that Hightower boy, but I suppose the basic premise is true."

"Oh, Mama." Sarah rose and folded her mother in a spontaneous hug. "I hope so."

Patricia grumbled and returned Sarah's hug with endearing awkwardness. For the first time in years, Sarah felt a glimmer of hope that the future would hold a better, kinder, more comfortable relationship for them.

Josh took Caitlin and J.J. to stay with Jennifer and Lucas while Sarah drove Patricia to Fargo and saw her settled into the rehabilitation center. The entire family was gathered on the front porch for an afternoon break when Sarah returned.

"Mommy! Mommy!" J.J. raced across the lawn and threw himself at her. Sarah caught him and swung him up into her arms, pretending to stagger under his weight.

"Wow! What's Jennifer been feeding you? I think you've gained ten pounds!"

"Nah." He giggled and planted a wet kiss on her cheek. "But we had a campfire last night and roasted hot dogs and made s'mores, and it was really fun."

Sarah searched the porch until she found Josh, leaning against a white post. His warm smile erased the fatigue of the long drive and she climbed the porch steps with renewed energy.

"They had fun, all right," Jennifer said dryly. "Both J.J. and Wayne had chocolate and marshmallow smeared from ear to ear."

Distracted by the welcoming heat in Josh's eyes, it took a moment for Sarah to realize what Jennifer was referring to. She swung J.J. to his feet and took the seat Josh held for her.

Josh settled his hands on her shoulders and leaned forward to whisper in her ear. "Want something cold to drink?"

She tipped her head back and looked up at him. "Yes, please."

He squeezed her shoulders in a gentle caress and walked to the end of the porch where a wicker table held tumblers and a pitcher of iced tea.

Murphy Redman sat next to Sarah in an old-fashioned grandfather rocker, a cane hooked over the arm, his leg stretched out in front of him with the foot propped on a small footstool.

"How are you, Murphy?" Sarah asked, assessing the healthy color in the older man's face and the sparkle in his deep black eyes.

"Fine, missy, just fine." He grinned at her and winked. "I'll be ready to dance at the Saddle Club this year, so you save a waltz for me. I'll be there to collect it."

"I'm going to hold you to that promise," she said, laughing.

J.J. and Wayne were seated on the porch steps, their swinging feet knocking their boot heels against the riser with rhythmic beats. Rum lay stretched full-length at the bottom of the steps, panting in the afternoon heat.

"You gotta have a daddy." Wayne's treble voice filled the silent space in adult conversation. "Who's your daddy?"

Sarah gasped, and her gaze shot to J.J.

"Why can't I just share yours?" J.J. asked with childish logic. "He's a pretty good one, isn't he?"

"Yeah, but he's mine." Wayne's tone left no doubt that sharing was out of the question. "You gotta have one of your own." He leaned closer to J.J. and stared, nose-to-nose. "How about Unca Josh? You live at the Rocking D where he lives. Is he your daddy?"

Sarah looked for Josh and found him standing perfectly still, staring at the two little boys, a glass of tea gripped in one hand. Her gaze flicked back to J.J. and she watched as he turned grave, uncertain eyes on Josh.

Josh moved, dropping on one knee next to the two solemn little boys.

"Yes, Wayne, I'm J.J.'s daddy. You're right.

Every boy has to have one of his own. And I'm his.''

A smile spread like sunshine over J.J.'s face and he bounced up, throwing himself at Josh with a crow of delight to wrap his arms around his neck. Josh caught the little boy in a bear hug, the glass he held falling to the wooden floor, spilling ice cubes amid a widening pool of cold tea.

The words were as solemn as a vow, the look on Josh's face filled with quiet, sure commitment. Sarah sniffed quietly, surreptitiously wiping telltale tears from her lashes. A swift, sideways glance told her that Jennifer, too, was blinking moisture from her eyes.

"Oh, for Pete's sake," Murphy snorted, thumping the floor with his cane. "Of course you're J.J.'s daddy. Any fool can see it—unless you're blind."

Josh looked over the blond silk of J.J.'s hair at Murphy. The disgusted look he got in return didn't clarify matters. "What are you talking about, Murphy?" he asked, puzzled.

"I'm talkin' about you bein' that little boy's daddy," Murphy declared. "He—heck, I knew he was a Hightower the minute I set eyes on him. He may have Sarah's hair, but he's got your eyes. That funny tiptilted lift at the outer corners and those coal black eyelashes—yup, they're your eyes, Josh. And the color's just like your mama's, green as grass." Murphy could remember Anna Hightower, but Josh couldn't. She'd deserted the family and left town when Josh was too young to remember her, and their father, enraged, had burned any belongings she'd left behind, together with any pictures of her. Tamping down old memories, Murphy repeated, "Like I said, any fool can see J.J.'s a Hightower."

Dumbfounded, Josh looked searchingly at J.J. The little boy had tilted his face back and was staring up at him. Not ten inches from Josh's own turquoise eyes, black-lashed emerald green stared back at him. Josh shook his head, hardly daring to believe the answer to J.J.'s parentage could be so simple and easy to read.

J.J. held tight in his arms, Josh turned slowly to look at his brother.

"Lucas?"

Lucas stared at the little boy in Josh's arms, his eyes narrowed as he assessed J.J.'s unique features. "You know," he said slowly, nodding, "I think Murphy's right. I've never seen eyes like that—except for ours."

Josh's gaze swung to Sarah. She was crying silently, one hand pressed against her lips. But a shaky smile fought to lift the corners of her mouth.

"Okay." J.J. patted Josh's cheek and demanded his attention. "Now I've got a daddy." At the bottom of the steps Rum surged to his feet, woofing deeply as a cat raced across the yard beyond the gate. J.J. wiggled and pushed against Josh's hold. "Wayne and I have to go see what scared the cat."

Josh swung him to his feet on the porch floor and the two little boys, oblivious to the adults' emotional upheaval, ran off into the yard, Rum loping at their heels, to investigate the cat.

Josh watched them go, moving only when Sarah walked across the porch and slid her arms around his waist. Neither of them was able to speak for the emotion that clogged their throats; Josh could only hold Sarah tight. In his arms stood the love he thought he'd lost forever, and racing laughing across the grass was the little boy he'd grown to love as his own.

"I'd still want to be his daddy even if Murphy hadn't said he was mine," he whispered unsteadily against her ear.

Sarah tipped her head back and smiled mistily up at him. "I know," she said softly.

Behind them, Jennifer sniffed and laughed. "I hope this means I get to plan a wedding," she said to Caitlin. "I just love weddings."

Caitlin eyed her doubtfully. "I've never been to a wedding."

"You'll like it." Lucas tugged the end of her ebony braid and grinned at her. "Weddings are just an excuse for a great big party. Takes Jennifer at least a month to plan one."

"I might not be here," the twelve-year-old said

fatalistically. "In another month I'll probably be back with my mom in L.A."

Sarah heard Caitlin's response and lifted her head from Josh's shoulder. She raised an eyebrow at him in inquiry and he nodded once, purposefully, determinedly.

"Caitlin," Sarah said, slipping out of Josh's arms to face the wide wicker chair where the girl sat. Josh shifted to stand just behind her, his hand resting possessively on her waist. "Josh and I have been meaning to talk to you about your going back to L.A. We don't want you to leave. We want you to stay here in Butte Creek, live with us and go to school."

Caitlin's eyes widened in surprise and she slowly lowered her feet to the porch, her hands gripping the wide arms of the chair. "You mean I'd stay here for school?"

"Yes, but not just for this year. We want you to live with us until you go off to college."

"Oh." The blaze of happiness that lit Caitlin's face swiftly faded. "My mom would never let me do that," she said with feigned indifference. "She says we're stuck with each other until I'm old enough to go to work."

Josh stiffened, his muscles bunching, flexing with anger. Sarah bit off the angry comment that trembled on her lips about her sister's stupidity.

"I've talked with Margaret," she said instead.

"She's agreed to let you stay with us, if you want to. Do you want to?"

The hard shell of indifference cracked, leaving pure happiness shining from Caitlin's green eyes, lifting her lips in a sweet smile of delight.

"Yes."

Sarah opened her arms, and Caitlin left the chair to slowly walk across the porch and be enfolded.

"You know," Josh observed reflectively, eyeing the twelve-year-old, "this means no more swearing until you go off to college. Do you think you can do that?"

"Sure," Caitlin answered blithely. "Piece of cake."

"What about shoveling manure?" he asked.

"Don't push your luck, *Unca* Josh," Caitlin responded, narrowing her eyes at him threateningly.

Behind them, Murphy and Lucas roared with laughter.

Sarah looked up at him, and Josh dropped a hard kiss against her mouth.

Josh had his heart back.

* * * * *

Share in the joy of yuletide romance with brand-new
stories by two of the genre's most beloved writers

DIANA PALMER
and
JOAN JOHNSTON
in

LONE ✦ STAR
CHRISTMAS

Diana Palmer and Joan Johnston share their favorite
Christmas anecdotes and personal stories in this
special hardbound edition.

Diana Palmer delivers an irresistible spin-off of her
LONG, TALL TEXANS series and Joan Johnston crafts an
unforgettable new chapter to **HAWK'S WAY** in this wonderful
keepsake edition celebrating the holiday season. So
perfect for gift giving, you'll want one for yourself...and
one to give to a special friend!

Available in November at your favorite retail outlet!

Only from

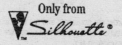

Silhouette®

Take 4 bestselling love stories FREE

Plus get a FREE surprise gift!

Special Limited-time Offer

Mail to Silhouette Reader Service™

3010 Walden Avenue
P.O. Box 1867
Buffalo, N.Y. 14240-1867

YES! Please send me 4 free Silhouette Special Edition® novels and my free surprise gift. Then send me 6 brand-new novels every month, which I will receive months before they appear in bookstores. Bill me at the low price of $3.34 each plus 25¢ delivery and applicable sales tax, if any.* That's the complete price and a savings of over 10% off the cover prices—quite a bargain! I understand that accepting the books and gift places me under no obligation ever to buy any books. I can always return a shipment and cancel at any time. Even if I never buy another book from Silhouette, the 4 free books and the surprise gift are mine to keep forever.

235 BPA A3UV

Name	(PLEASE PRINT)	

Address	Apt. No.	

City	State	Zip

This offer is limited to one order per household and not valid to present Silhouette Special Edition® subscribers. *Terms and prices are subject to change without notice. Sales tax applicable in N.Y.

USPED-696

©1990 Harlequin Enterprises Limited

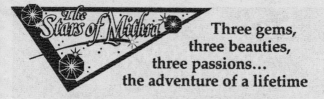

Silhouette Women Know Romance When They See It.

And they'll see it on **ROMANCE CLASSICS**, the new 24-hour TV channel devoted to romantic movies and original programs like the special **Romantically Speaking—Harlequin™ Goes Prime Time**.

Romantically Speaking—Harlequin™ Goes Prime Time introduces you to many of your favorite romance authors in a program developed exclusively for Harlequin® and Silhouette® readers.

Watch for **Romantically Speaking—Harlequin™ Goes Prime Time** beginning in the summer of 1997.

*If you're not receiving **ROMANCE CLASSICS**, call your local cable operator or satellite provider and ask for it today!*

ROMANCE CLASSICS

Escape to the network of your dreams.

See Ingrid Bergman and Gregory Peck in *Spellbound* on Romance Classics.

#1135 WHITE WOLF—Lindsay McKenna
That Special Woman!
Hardened corporate raider Dain Phillips turned to mystical medicine woman Erin Wolf for a "miracle" cure. But he never expected to care so deeply for Erin—or that her spiritual healing would forever alter him body and soul!

#1136 THE RANCHER AND THE SCHOOLMARM—
Penny Richards
Switched at Birth
Schoolteacher Georgia Williams was stunned when her fiancé passed her in the airport, got attacked and suffered amnesia. How would she handle the revelation that this riveting man who stole her heart was *not* her groom-to-be—but instead his long-lost identical twin?

#1137 A COWBOY'S TEARS—Anne McAllister
Code of the West
Mace and Jenny Nichols had the *perfect* marriage—until Mace discovered some sad news. Jenny was determined to convince her brooding cowboy of her unfaltering love—and that there was more than one way to capture their dreams....

#1138 THE PATERNITY TEST—Pamela Toth
Powerful Nick Kincaid could handle anything—except his mischievous twins. His new nanny, Cassie Wainright, could handle everything—except her attraction to Nick. Now Cassie was pregnant, and Nick was being put to the *ultimate* test.

#1139 HUSBAND: BOUGHT AND PAID FOR—Laurie Paige
Fearing for her life, heiress Jessica Lockhart hired P.I. Brody Smith—and then proposed marriage. Her aloof bodyguard agreed to a platonic union, but that didn't mean the lovely lady had the right to wiggle her way into his heart...

#1140 MOUNTAIN MAN—Doris Rangel
Gloria Pellman was a single mom, raising her young son, Jamey—alone, thank you very much! She didn't need a husband! But when Hank Mason rescued them from his rugged mountain, Jamey discovered a friend...and Gloria discovered her heart was in danger!

Daniel MacGregor is at it again…

New York Times bestselling author

NORA ROBERTS

introduces us to a new generation of MacGregors
as the lovable patriarch of the illustrious MacGregor
clan plays matchmaker again, this time to his three
gorgeous granddaughters in

THE MacGREGOR BRIDES

From Silhouette Books

Don't miss this brand-new continuation of Nora Roberts's
enormously popular *MacGregor* miniseries.

Available November 1997 at your favorite retail outlet.

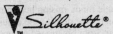